ALSO BY RON SMITH

POETRY

Seasonal
A Buddha Named Baudelaire
Enchantment & Other Demons

FICTION

Rainshadow: Stories From Vancouver Island
(Edited with Steven Guppy)

WHAT MEN KNOW ABOUT WOMEN

WHAT MEN KNOW
About Women

STORIES BY

Ron Smith

OOLICHAN BOOKS
LANTZVILLE, BRITISH COLUMBIA, CANADA
1999

Canadian Cataloguing in Publication Data

Smith, Ron, 1943-
    What men know about women

ISBN 0-88982-183-6 (bound) - ISBN 0-88982-177-1 (pbk.)

    I. Title.
PS8587.M5838W52 1999   C813'.54   C99-910647-3
PR9199.3.S5518W52 1999

We gratefully acknowledge the support of the Canada Council
for the Arts for our publishing program.

THE CANADA COUNCIL | LE CONSEIL DES ARTS
FOR THE ARTS | DU CANADA
SINCE 1957 | DEPUIS 1957

Grateful acknowledgement is also made to the BC Ministry of
Tourism, Small Business and Culture for their financial support.

We acknowledge the financial support of the Government of
Canada through the Book Publishing Industry Development
Program for our publishing activities.

Canadä

Cover photo by VCG/FPG-CANADA INC.

Published by
Oolichan Books
P.O. Box 10, Lantzville
British Columbia, Canada
V0R 2H0

Printed in Canada

For
Gary Geddes

For Edwin and Mary Webb
Mark and Printha Ellis
Brian and Hazel Barnes

and, as always,
for Pat

Contents

A man is granted two wishes by the little people. For his first wish he asks for a bottle of whiskey that will always be full. He takes a sip and the bottle immediately refills. He takes another sip and once again the bottle fills. He is delighted with his good fortune, but as with all magic he fears there might be a trick or deception, the bottle might be made to disappear, or he might be a participant in a fleeting dream or pleasant illusion, so when asked to make his second wish, the man hesitates, looks about for reassurance, then says, Just to be on the safe side, I'll have another one of those.

Desire is a bottle that never empties.

The Silver Fox

Sometimes stories, to be heard, burst from the rocks where they are hidden.

Once there was a Silver Fox. She was a beautiful animal. She had soft, silky fur, bright eyes that shone like the stars in a dark sky, good white teeth, and strong legs like the willow. She kept herself very clean, always took care of herself. She was very beautiful. One day she decided she would like to throw a party for all her friends in the forest but she didn't have enough food or drink, so she made a plan. She went to the road where the humans passed along in their wagons and she rolled in the dirt and mud. She beat herself with a stick just hard enough to make bruises and draw blood and then she lay down in the middle of the road. Soon some humans, a man and a woman, came along the road in their wagon, and when they saw the Silver Fox lying in the middle of the road they stopped and the man got down and lifted the Silver Fox gently up to his wife who took her best comb from her basket and combed the mud and dust from the Silver Fox's fur. The man went to the creek that runs not far from the road and brought back water for the Silver Fox to drink and water to touch and clean her bruises and cuts.

Poor beautiful little creature, said the woman.

Yes, said the man, she is beautiful. But she looks better already for your care.

He then took the Silver Fox from the woman and carefully placed the Silver Fox on some blankets in the back of the wagon. He turned to his horses and they started off down the road. For a short while the Silver Fox lay quietly in the back, resting until she was certain the humans would no longer turn to see how she was keeping. She shut her eyes and pretended to sleep. After a little while she began to throw the provisions—meat, fruit, potatoes, bread, wine, cheese, grains—from the wagon out on to the side of the road. When she had enough food and drink for her party, she jumped quietly from the wagon, ran back along the road and gathered up everything. Back at her den she cooked a great meal and invited all her friends to share in her wealth.

Now, a big Grey Wolf was invited to the party, and he was very impressed by what the Silver Fox had prepared for all her friends. He decided he, too, wanted to have a party for the people of the forest and he asked Silver Fox how she had managed to find so much food and drink. Silver Fox told him the story, and the next day Grey Wolf went down to the road that the humans travelled. He rolled in the dust and mud and he beat himself with a stick just hard enough to make bruises and to draw a little blood. He then lay down in the middle of the road and waited for the wagon loaded with food and drink. Shortly he could hear the sounds of horse's hooves and he lay very quiet and still, almost as if he were dead. The wagon stopped and from the corner of his eye he could see the man jump down from the wagon. The man moved closer and the big Grey Wolf waited for the man to lift him up to his wife and for her to comb the mud from his fur. How ugly he must appear, he thought, but soon his fur would glisten from the woman's combing. But instead the man kicked him in the side, hard with his boot, and then kicked him again and again, first in the side, then in the head, and then in the rear end.

It's just an ugly old wolf, said the man, a big, ugly Grey Wolf.

The man then lifted the Grey Wolf by his tail and hit him hard against a tree and then threw him into the ditch at the side of the road. The man climbed back into the wagon and drove his team of horses off down the road and the big Grey Wolf could hear them both laugh in disgust as they disappeared around a bend.

Sometimes stories are a path to the heart. Other times they show us our place in the world. Like dreaming eyes refusing the darkness of sleep.

What I'm Asking

We are speaking of conquests.

When we reached the top of Pendle, Arnie says, when we passed over the last ledge after the long hike up, that's when we found it.

Just like that, without the slightest warning, when me and the two lads were out of breath from charging the last forty, maybe fifty, feet to the summit—me pushing the boys, them scrambling ahead of me, the two set to win the day—that's when we stumbled onto the body.

This was no laughing matter, he says, his lips curling as he lifts his pint. No laughing matter at all, and that's the truth.

We all drink.

It's just after five-thirty in the evening and people are beginning to trickle into the pub. The four of us—Busie, Pope, Arnie and me—take our place at one end of the bar, near a set of taps, three tall white-marble handles. We watch Nigel, the barman, pull us four fresh pints. He takes considerable care, I notice, topping up each one. Listening. I sit on one of two barstools and look back over Busie's shoulder at the shafts of light coming through the frosted and stained-glass windows—red roses set against a soft, pale yellow.

These are not like your lot, Arnie continues, looking directly at me. Not like the Rockies. These are only hills really. But rugged all the same. Enough to wear the leather off a good pair of boots. What tracks there are are built for sheep.

He pauses. I watch his movements in the mirror behind the row of liquor bottles. People from the village, some of whom I've seen earlier in the day, pack around us. I can hear Arnie's breathing, he is getting that close.

A challenge even for the likes of you, he says.

He leans one elbow on the bar and studies me from the side. He waits, hoping, wanting me to speak. But I'm not going to be trapped. Not this time. Then he laughs, straightens up and thrusts his hands into his pockets.

Get on with it, Busie says, don't be baiting the guest.

I had flown over to Manchester with my wife and two daughters to attend Busie's daughter's wedding. But I doubt Busie is defending me. Arnie and he are close friends. Tight. And I know from past visits that Arnie considers me an overweight, stressed-out North American. He said as much once before when he challenged me to join him on a climb of Mount Helvellyn in the

Lake District. I declined. Mandy, Busie's wife, says Arnie's fit as a butcher's dog. But when I look at Arnie what I see in the mirror is a short, bald man. Red faced. An upholsterer, who dresses in dark blue coveralls. His hands are delicate although when we first met I remember being surprised at the strength of his grip.

Pope takes out a cigarette and rolls it between the tips of his fingers. Thinking. Then he puts it in his mouth and lights it. He says, That's not how you told the story last time. Not at all. Last time you discovered the body on the way down. Pope's fingers toy with his scimpy moustache and beard. He has black, curly hair and cultivates his resemblance to Bob Dylan.

Arnie lifts his mug and drains off the beer. He takes several deep breaths and raps the bar.

That's right, Arnie says, that's right. The poet plumber is right again. Time passes and I forget the most important details.

Sweat beads on his forehead and large nose. He removes a hankerchief from his pocket and wipes his face and head, then, while looking around the pub, nods, as if affirming that this is his stage, his show.

For once Pope's not 'blowin in the wind'. He's right, Arnie says. He's got it bloody right. He stares at me since I'm the only one who hasn't heard the story. Comes from paying attention. Ain't that right, Pope? he says. Sorry, he says to me. I'd best back up and tell things the way they actually happened.

He pauses and blows air out, making a whistling sound with his lips. Then he coughs, clearing his throat.

While I listen to Arnie talk I remember what my wife

Corrie said. Arnie may have the gift of the gab—she said this tongue in cheek, with a sense of irony that at first I missed—but he's also an A-1 bullshitter. Corrie recognizes bullshit for what it is. She's trying to caution me. Women in general, I suspect, detect bullshit faster than men do. I'm not sure why this is so.

Anyway, Corrie says she thinks he's one of those people who thrives on unhappiness, not because he's one of those gloomy types who considers unhappiness the only indisputable state of the human condition but because he sees nothing sporting in talking about those who're merely satisfied or happy with their existence. I think her assessment of Arnie a bit harsh, but recently my own life has been moving at such a crawl that I find I'm no longer the best judge of character. Now I'm tempted to chuckle, to let Arnie know I'm on to him, but he's already in full stride.

When we reached the top, he says, exhausted as we were, we saw this bloke sat there, slump shouldered, his head pitched toward ground. As if sleeping. We passed him by and continued on to the high point. To the top of the world, like. For years I'd promised to take the lads up there. To a place where they could look down on their home. And beyond. Where they could see something more grand than stone walls, terraced housing and the reservoir. Where they could see there is a world beyond Barrowford and the fields we'd walked.

Nigel pulls us four more pints and then pulls several more and asks us to pass them along to those who are jammed in behind. Hands reach forward and I hear one

24

voice after another say Ta, like we're a choreographed scene out of Chaplin's *Modern Times*.

The women, Corrie included, move off to the other end of the bar when Arnie launches into his story, and soon they start talking with a few of the lads who've just come in from a local rugby match.

That must have been quite a thrill, Pope interrupts. I remember my first and last climb up Pendle. With the old man. Cut from the same cloth, you two. I was sick for days.

Some things never change, Busie says and shrugs.

Arnie grins and wags his head. As I say, he says, we'd walked right past him—the dead bloke, I mean—on our way up. Didn't want to disturb someone so deep in meditation. Besides, the boys were too tired and cold, not to mention relieved, to give a damn about some old guy perched on a mountain peak. After a quick look around, they found a sheltered spot in amongst the rocks. Huddled against the wind and mist, they opened their packs and dug out buttered bread and jam. I poured each of them a cup of tea from my thermos and then suggested we catch our breath and start back down, before the cloud cover settled in.

Arnie fidgets. Foam lines his upper lip, highlighting his smile. I'm tempted to say he looks like a clown, but he gives his lips a smack and sweeps the thin white moustache away with his tongue before I can say anything.

He continues, This time when we passed the bloke I said, Hello. When he didn't reply I thought I'd best have a closer look. I bent over and bellowed in his ear.

25

Up close. You all right mate? Too bloody cold to be sat here, I said. Some people can be hard work. He didn't budge. When I shook his shoulder, he fell over. He was frozen stiff. Rigor mortis. A flask was stuck between his thighs. The boys gawked. What's wrong with him? they asked. I stepped back and removed my cap, out of habit as much as anything else. Although I didn't want to frighten the lads, I knew there was no way round the truth. Dead, I said. I reckon he's dead. He's up and died, I told them.

Pope chuckles. Up and died! he repeats, sticking his thumbs into his black vest. You have a grand way with words, my friend. As Bob Dylan says, "Everybody sees hisself walking around with no one else." Mighty fine words, indeed. The boys must've been reassured by your touching explanation.

Arnie wipes his forehead with his sleeve. He is pleased with himself. Evidently he takes what Pope has said as a compliment. He turns to Nigel, makes a circle in the air with his hand, and orders another round. On him, he says, and points his finger towards me. It's about time our guest paid his dues. Now where was I?

The body, Busie says, you finally have the body. You are making hard work of it this time! You know that? He slumps back in his stool. Come on, out with it, before we're all taken up by your friend rigor mortis.

We all laugh and lift our glasses.

Arnie stretches and rocks back on his heels.

Well, as everyone can appreciate, the boys were in shock. I told them we had a moral obligation to report our discovery to the police. We made a quick descent to where we parked the car and drove the last few miles to the police station. By this time cold were really eating into our bones. November! Arnie shudders and takes a large mouthful of beer. The lads were shivering and all police could think about were me filling in bloody forms.

Busie edges up in his seat, as if he's been given a cue to speak. There are them whose job it is, he says slowly, to ask others to fill in pieces of paper that aren't yet full. Busie's Law, he says. Never fails. He places his hands behind his head and leans back. Never fails.

Arnie sighs and his mouth quivers like a cat sighting a bird.

And that's precisely the point I tried to make with them, Arnie says. Speaking of making a day's work out of nought, I'll tell you! I nodded in direction of lads and said I hoped they wouldn't be catching their death of cold. I might as well have been talking to sheep for all the notice them two coppers took.

Diplomatic, Busie says, as they usually are.

Arnie says, I asked what about him that's at the top, and their faces were blank as two sheets of foolscap. The dead man, I said. He'll be all right, they said. If what you say is true, he'll be going nowhere. Geniuses, I wanted to say.

Laughter comes from the direction of the dart board and for a moment Arnie looks distracted. Angry at the interruption. Almost as if he wants to fight someone. He has been put off his rhythm. He stands up on his toes and stares behind us, over his shoulder. I can see a small nerve near his left eye begin to twitch, and his hands tremble. Then he takes a deep breath and smiles, his sincerity as ripe as last year's peaches. The colour has gone out of the stained-glass window.

So I filled in bloody forms, Arnie says, describing what they already knew. What we'd seen and already told them. Everything in duplicate. Weren't that much to say, really. It was then they served the knockout punch. Just when I was telling lads we could go, the older cop said they needed us to show them way to dead bloke. How many dead bodies you expect to find on a Sunday afternoon on top of Pendle? I asked. Again they stone-walled me. The younger one asked if I were trying to be amusing. A smart ass, you mean? I asked. And when he nodded, I said, Not at all, furthest thing from my mind, I said. Sod that. It's the lads, I said. My boys. Who'll pay the piper when they both come down with pneumonia? I asked. Who'll pay for boot leather? Not you sorry lot, I said, that's for sure. The taxpayer, I told them. Me, Arnie Henderson, I said, in case they missed my point.

Taxes and Arnie Henderson, Pope says. Oil and water. Wine and vinegar. Quite a combination. He pauses and pulls a face, the corners of his mouth drawn down, his eyelids half closed. Arnie Henderson paying taxes! When did this sad story begin?

Arnie looks at him. He holds his beer in one hand while he clenches and unclenches the other. Smoke from Pope's cigarette, which sits on the edge of the ashtray, rises and circles Arnie's head. With his free hand, Arnie stubs out the cigarette vigorously. Pope's mouth opens and closes, but he says nothing.

If truth be known, Arnie says, the lads were only too happy to cooperate. For them this were an adventure. More exciting than the climb itself. He continues to stare at Pope, studying his face, as if trying to bring his features into focus, as if trying to place somebody he thinks he recognizes. I'd be dishonest, he says, if I didn't say I was disappointed.

Besides, Busie says, you couldn't very well tell folk that all you wanted to do was lead an expedition to nearest pub. Now could you?

We all laugh.

True enough, Arnie concedes. And those two coppers, well, stuck in pig shit they were. They insisted the three of us accompany them to where the body was. That way we could verify each other's story and be done with the matter. What a load of rubbish! It was then I made my last pitch. Whilst I didn't like to get mixed up in someone else's affairs, death is everybody's business, I told them.

You try to do the right thing, Busie says, and sure enough someone will have a go at you. There's always someone cocksure enough willing to tell you you've got it all wrong. Busie's Law. He folds his arms across his chest and says, If anything can go wrong, it will. Credit Murphy with that one!

And it did, Arnie says. We climbed to the top of Pendle, for the second time that day, my legs as weary as water. And when we got there, dead bloke were gone! Can you imagine that? No bloody body! He'd disappeared! Up and walked away! Just like that! Nothing! Not even the flask! The police were right pissed off, to say the least. I said, Maybe I were wrong. Maybe bloke were only sleeping.

Arnie stops and runs his hand back and forth across his head, as if he is massaging his thoughts, as if stroking the skin might encourage an idea to pop out of his mouth like a genie. Light has gone from the window.

As I see it, something on top of that mountain had scared Arnie. I figured he'd stared death in the face and found a force that was impenetrable. Hidden. And was best left so. He shrugs his shoulders inside his coveralls, like he's trying to slough off some huge unmanageable weight. He gives a little laugh and then looks at me as if I'm the only one in the room. As if my sole purpose in being there is to vex him. Then he glances from face to face.

He says, We're not to be judged by the stories we tell. Right?

Nor by the company we keep, Pope says.

This isn't a court of law. Right?

Only for them who lives in glass houses, Busie says.

Arnie is pleased. He has us back on side.

I had to confess I hadn't tried to find a pulse, he says. One of the coppers accused me of making the whole thing up. Can you fathom that! And the other one said some people would go to any lengths to impress their kids. Me lads stuck up for me right quick. But the one cop, the older guy, wanted to get his licks in. I'd obviously rubbed him the wrong way. He told me there were serious penalties for filing false reports.

Charming, Busie says. He glances at each one of us, yawns, then blinks and closes his eyes. Charming, he repeats softly. Someone needs to sort out that lot. There's no mystery in all of this, is there? he says. Arnie hesitates, expecting Busie to answer his own question, but he is silent. We wait. Finally he opens his eyes, scratches his beard and says, No mystery. And there's the pity.

Bleeding paper shufflers is all, Arnie says and continues. We were dog tired by now. And the light were rapidly disappearing out of sky. We dragged ourselves back down Pendle to police car. I were beginning to feel like that bloke who pushes stone up hill, only to have it roll back down to bottom.

Sisyphus, Pope answers.

Whoever, Arnie says. I tried to tell the cops it all had to do with bad luck. Nothing had gone right in last few days. Between the headlamps the road looked narrower than I remembered. And as we came around a tight corner, we almost ran up tail pipe of an army convoy. An officer waved us over and stuck his head in the window. We've got a problem here, he said. Your jurisdiction. We were on manoeuvres at the top of Pendle earlier this afternoon and found a body.

Needless to say I could have kissed that ugly bugger right on his big, fat arse, Arnie gloats.

Gentleman was on his side, the officer continued, knotted up like a pretzel. Medics examined him and were certain he'd died of an heart attack. Otherwise we wouldn't have moved him. He's in the back of the forward truck there.

Well, Arnie says, our two coppers looked like they'd lost the F.A. Cup in a shootout. The five of us followed the Captain to his truck and the lads and I identified the body as bloke we'd seen up Pendle. Are you certain, the younger policeman asked. As I am of me own mother, I said. The boys nodded.

Who was it? someone asks from behind me.

No idea, Arnie says. No idea who he was. I searched local papers for the next few days, but no mention was made of the incident. Expected to find a reference to lads and me, to be quite honest. Not a thing. It were as if it never happened.

The pub seems suddenly very quiet.

No one likes to stumble on the dead, I reckon. Even in a story.

So what's the lesson, I ask.

Next time I climb a mountain, Arnie says, not looking at me, not wanting to acknowledge the question I'm asking, and see a fella sat there taking in the view—here he pauses for effect—I'll tip me hat, wish him top of day and let him be.

Easily fooled, someone says from the back of the crowd, but never a fool. That's our Arnie. Everyone laughs, but with an uneasiness that causes me to shiver.

Against the wainscotting, the lamplight in the pub washes warm.

That's not quite what I meant, I say.

I want to know what it would be like to discover someone that way. To stumble on a body.

I guess what I meant, I say, is, what did you feel?

As I see it, Arnie's always chewing on the raw end of

emotion, determined to prove something, although what exactly is unclear to me. God knows, we all need to feel that we matter, that we're in some way important. The way our paths cross is random enough. Perhaps this is why we tell stories. I don't know.

What do you mean? Arnie's voice rises, his cheeks puffing out, red.

About the dead guy, I say. What did you feel about the dead guy?

What are you getting at?

I can see Arnie's upset. Peeved. He's breathing harder and shifting on his feet. His hands circle through the air, like he's directing traffic. He bites his lip and twists around to look at Pope and Busie.

I felt sorry for the bloke, he says. All alone up there. Cold. Christ it was cold. Freezing bloody cold. He pauses, as if his own breath has suddenly been squeezed out of him. He says, Besides, I don't like looking on the dead. Gives me the creeps. He pauses. It's hard to describe, he says. Sure I felt something. I'm not a bleeding robot! He looks down at his feet. The lads were hungry. Then he closes his eyes and brings the fingertips of both hands together at his lips. All I wanted to do was get to a pub, have a pint and forget what I'd seen. Is that what you want to hear?

So that's it?

I hunch forward. I'm trying not to judge here, not blame anyone for anything.

That's it! he says, glaring at me.

Arnie seems puzzled. He looks straight into my eyes and then at my mouth, as if looking beyond my teeth for my tongue. I didn't know the bloke from Adam, he says. How do you feel something for someone you don't know?

I take a mouthful of beer. I want to say, There has to be a way.

We are all silent.

The noise of the pub, the voices and laughter, the music and click of the pool balls, gets louder.

Busie, staring down at the bar, says, For every problem you solve, you create two more. That's the way it is with people. Nothing ever changes. He picks up his empty glass and lifts it to his lips. Busie's law, he says.

Everyone shuffles. No one looks at anyone else. Instead they watch Nigel pulling beer, at bottles arranged on shelves below the opposite counter, at photographs hanging on the walls, shots of the village, under water, during the torrential flood of the fifties. And they nod.

Someone switches on the TV. Heads turn and everyone looks at the picture showing highlights from the Brazilian Grand Prix.

Busie is right of course. But I want things to be different. I want him to be wrong. I want to say, If fate connects us, it also keeps us separate. And I want to say to Arnie, I know you know exactly what I'm asking.

But like everyone else, I watch cars speed around the track in the heat of that southern sun. And I wonder if we are all waiting with the same sense of exhilaration and dread for one driver—just one, alone—to take that little extra risk.

Desire

For a lark, because we had nothing better to do, a friend, Karl Singer, and I stood in the middle of the pavement at the corner of Granville and Georgia, two main thoroughfares in Vancouver, and looked up into the sky. At nothing. The old clock that had stood at this intersection for years ticked on; people late for work or hurrying to business appointments detoured around us, some throwing us hostile glances for causing them to swerve off an otherwise purposeful course; and every now and again a driver honked his horn in a blast of irritation— whether at us or at another driver, I wasn't sure.

I noticed the mountains on the North Shore had finally lost their cap of snow in the heat of the summer sun. And at the foot of Granville, I could make out whitecaps on the inlet and the funnels and flags of cruise ships. For a moment I speculated on the journeys people take, how ships that put out to sea must become prisons of hospitality, floating islands of desire.

We continued to scan the sky, a deep and luminous blue beyond the thrust of the skyscrapers. Shadows filled the length of both streets and a gentle breeze, like a ghost's breath, made the midmorning air feel cooler than it really was. At intervals, sunlight would suddenly strike a face and the person's hand would shoot up to shield his eyes. Or brilliant light would bounce off a shop window, the glare blinding, leaving little sunspots dancing in your eyes. Karl stretched his right arm upward, his jacket sleeve falling back and forming a cowl around his shoulder. He pointed with his index finger towards the sky. Immediately I thought he looked as if he should have been turned the other way round and painted on a chapel ceiling, his movement was so sudden and authoritative, so self-assured, his limb seemingly detached from his body.

I peered up, my gaze following the direction of his arm, and nodded. I saw nothing, although instinctively I felt I must, even if only for an instant. By now my head was tilted so far back I feared I might lose my balance. Besides a certain degree of discomfort, I felt disoriented. Perhaps I did see a flash of light, something, anything, a daymoon faintly visible against a blue sky, the lonely orbit of an astronaut, a soul winging its way to heaven, that held my attention. After all, I was one of the architects of this scheme, not one of its dupes.

A man wearing a finely tailored, three-piece suit was the first to stop and join us. His curiosity was palpable. He set his leather briefcase down and immediately pointed his arm in the air. I looked at him in disbelief and then cast my eyes once again towards the sky. What was it he saw, I wondered?

Then an older, heavy-set woman, wearing a thick winter coat and a hat with a veil, almost knocked me over. She was so busy looking skyward, she miscalculated her steps and tripped on the curb.

What's up? she asked, stumbling and grabbing my sweater to steady herself.

I pointed, somewhat less enthusiastically than Karl or the man in the suit had, towards the sky.

Oh, she said, that's beautiful. Quite remarkable, don't you think? Her neck made accordian folds as she arched her back and brushed the black net away from her eyes and off her forehead.

I mumbled something unintelligible at her. Now there were three of them who saw whatever it was I was unable to see.

The cooling breeze died. Kitty-corner from us a small band of street musicians packed up their instruments and, like a family of gypsy street thugs, moved between the cars towards us, their fingers strumming the shadows.

The sun had shifted higher into the sky and the light reflecting off the buildings was dazzling.

Two young women came strolling along, arm in arm. They were dressed in bright, summer-coloured suits with short skirts. Their lips were full and moist and laughing. When they tipped their heads and squinted their eyes gazing up into the sky, their long golden and auburn hair cascaded down their backs and brushed against the smalls of their arched backs. They jostled against Karl, who pretended not to notice them, but then nestled closer to them with his hips and legs and whispered something I was unable to hear. Their mouths made perfect "O"s. I gaped in amazement and thought to admonish him, but I was certain he knew how much I feared making a fool of myself with a woman.

The man wearing the suit rubbed the toe of his shoe on the back of his pant leg, shifting from one foot to the other, never once looking away from whatever held his gaze.

Soon, others joined us and we became a crowd of twenty or more people. We all stood on that spot, at that corner, looking up into the sky. At nothing, as far as I could see! The hands of the old clock rested on twelve.

Some pointed to objects they saw, confident of their vision. They reported cloud formations in the shapes of sheep or ships or unicorns or gods of whatever design filled their minds. They saw birds—swallows, pigeons, crows, sparrows—circle and dive between the buildings that fashioned the canyon floor where we stood. They saw aircraft. And a few saw an inexplicable light.

For a time I was skeptical about what they said they saw, especially when I watched a woman lean out a window eight floors up and empty a pitcher of water into the sky above our heads, but with time I was convinced that what they said they saw, I, too, could see, with a little effort.

As hard as I concentrated, all I got for my exertion was a headache.

At that moment, just when I thought my neck would permanently kink from straining to look at the heavens, a young redhead tapped me on the shoulder. Her face was sprinkled with freckles.

I've been watching you, she said.

A trolley bus passed by noiselessly. A cyclist wheeled around the corner, his legs pumping effortlessly.

What is it you desire, she asked, really desire?

Oh, I said, because I did not know her, a little of this, a little of that.

I see, she said. I've been watching you from the start, from when you first took up your position on the corner. I know what you and your friend are up to.

I pretended not to understand what she was saying. As sore as my neck was, I leaned back and looked up once again into the sky.

Don't treat me like the others, she said.

She was tall. Her long fingers caressed the surface of a locket she wore around her neck. With me, she said, there is a difference between what you think you can do and what can be done. If you want to kiss me, go ahead! Don't just think about it! Otherwise all you have is the thought.

Words rolled around in her mouth like hard toffee.

She pressed the clasp on the locket and opened it.

What do you see, she asked?

Nothing, I said.

No, no, she said. Her eyes were blue and endless, and her voice wrapped around me, lingering. You must look more carefully. More closely.

I did.

And what I thought I saw was a tiny mosaic insert that in the flickering sunlight of the street looked like a portrait of me.

The Last Time We Talked

Larry sits across from me at lunch and I know he's thinking much the same as I am. What the hell's happened to this guy over the last sixteen years?

He takes a sip from his water and then watches the ice cubes swirl around the glass. I'm taking in my usual overdose of caffeine, spiked with too much sugar and cream. At least I've quit smoking.

He's asking himself the obvious things: Do I look as bad as he does? Do I look as old? I know I haven't lost as much hair or put on as much weight. He's thinking: The guy's a lard ass. And his wife, what about his wife? She was attractive back then. What's she look like now? Could she possibly look as tired, as worn down as he does? He's asking himself about my wife, my Annie, which kind of pisses me off.

I look at my hands. No calluses. My hands are soft and pink, fleshy, and my life line forks in the middle of my palm. I used to move around the squash court like a tomcat. Now I can't roll off my couch without feeling winded. I admit it, I'm in rotten shape.

There's nothing subtle about the way we look at each other. Sixteen years will do that to your perspective. I look, but I don't see. This is not someone I know, not quite. I watch him closely. I want to see more than some physical similarities to the memory I'm dredging up. Hell, I have enough trouble with the picture I see of myself when I look at the wedding photograph Annie keeps on the mantlepiece.

But Larry and I had been good friends. When we went for a beer after an hour of squash, we always had something to say to each other. Small talk mostly, about sports or music. Occasionally, when one of us needed help, we'd confide in the other.

As I say, we were friends. When the four of us played Canasta and drank gin into the early hours of the morning—well, there wasn't a topic that made any one of us blush. I'm hoping that history will help get us over this initial shock.

How's Carla? I ask.

He sucks in some air, looks me straight in the eye and says nothing. He drops his gaze to the menu and recites the entrees, as if I'm retarded.

I had talked to Carla two nights earlier, shortly after I'd arrived at the detox centre. I checked in, got the schedule for meals and sessions, and then the lecture on curfew and booze from a short, stout woman who made it clear I wasn't going to jerk her around. Her eyes were huge. All the rules were for my benefit, she pointed out.

I agreed. I assumed this would show I was going to be cooperative. Receptive to the therapy.

After I'd unpacked my gear, I sprawled out on one of the three narrow beds in the room. I studied the ceiling and thought, this is not going to be easy. This is prison. With day passes handed out at the discretion of the warden I'd just met. And worst of all, I'd volunteered myself for this experiment. So far I was lucky, no one had showed up to share my room. Or toilet and shower. This would be a bonus, to be on my own. When I broke into the sweats, I could deal with my demons alone. The idea of sharing my paranoia with someone else made me feel unclean. Besides, I figured if I could stand two weeks of looking at the photo wallboard someone had used to decorate the room, I'd probably survive the cure.

Everyone had insisted I try therapy. Group therapy, for Christ's sake. I don't much like talking about myself, at least not about the intimate stuff. And especially not to a bunch of strangers. Still, I knew as well as anyone else that I needed to get my life back on track. The last two flashes of temper had scared the shit out of me. Smashing crockery was one thing, but when you started to grab family around the neck, well, crazy came to mind. That's what hurt. The striking out. Wondering if I might bust someone's head open.

The ceiling was made up of two hundred and sixteen one-foot by one-foot tiles. I tried to calculate the dimensions of the room but I'd never been much good at math. Then I lay perfectly still and listened to my breathing. As my chest rose and fell, I thought about phoning Larry and Carla. I tried to understand the connection between my counting, my breathing, and them, but I couldn't see one. What a waste of time, I decided. The mind just works that way sometimes.

Larry and Carla had moved from the city up to this small town on the Sunshine Coast a few months after Annie and I moved to Vancouver Island. Larry had landed some work on a new television series. Before that he had done some free-lancing on major films. But the work was intermittent and this series promised something more steady. The script called for a small seaside town with an active harbour. Larry discovered Gibsons. At least the producers credited him with the discovery. And that was enough to guarantee him employment for as long as the show ran.

Just before we left, Carla had become seriously ill. After a couple of weeks of tests, no one seemed able to diagnose her problem. The doctors advised hospitalization. Still no one knew what was wrong with her. We could see the lesions developing up and down her arms and legs but no one could stop them. The wounds spread and grew. They turned dark brown and then black. They looked like craters in her skin. She had been so beautiful, Annie said. Specialists were flown in from the Mayo Clinic and some place in Florida. Nothing changed. We visited her a few times in hospital, but the sight of her turned my stomach. Annie's, too, although on the last visit I was surprised when Annie bent down to the bed and held Carla in her arms. The two of them rocked back and forth. Whispering. Sobbing. Annie stroking Carla's hair. Once we'd settled on the Island, the separation grew into silence. Neither Annie nor I had the words.

Later we heard Carla had been released from St. Paul's and they had moved. Here. When I suggested to Annie that I might look them up, she had said, Are you sure? Do you think you should? After all this time? Christ, Axel, she might have died! It's been sixteen years! What will you say to Lar if she's dead?

Sorry? I had asked, a little too sarcastically.

Annie had made a fist.

I'll tell him I'm sorry. What else would you have me say?

Annie had been right. Getting up the nerve to make the phone call had been harder than I thought it would be.

I climbed off the bed, put on a clean shirt and made my way to the office. Three men and a woman sat in the large stuffed chairs in the common area toward which all the rooms faced. The woman said something about taking chances but the context was lost on me. One of the men smiled in my direction as I walked by, but all I could think about was the phone call. The warden sat behind her desk. She looked downright unfriendly. Her hair was grey and knotted up in a bun at the back.

I rapped lightly on the doorjamb and said, Excuse me. Have you got a phone?

We both stared at the phone on her desk.

There are pay phones in the entrance, she said. All clients are required to use the pay phones.

I turned and looked down the hall. I could see the phones in their little cubicles but no phone books.

Sorry to bother you again, I said, but I don't have the number.

She squeezed her lips tight, reached into a drawer and placed a phone book on her desk. Her chubby hand rested on the cover. These have a way of walking out of here, she said. So it doesn't leave the room. Understand?

I nodded. Charmer, I wanted to say.

I had stewed over the thought of making this phone call for a couple of weeks. Now I had to fight to get the number. I flipped through the pages to the M's. I half expected not to find the name. But there it was. L. J. McCormack. And the number. Perhaps it was a coincidence. I had never known Larry's middle initial. This could be somebody else altogether. The name's not that uncommon, I thought.

The warden placed a pen and pad of paper in front of me. I wanted to tell this sweetheart to mind her own business. I wanted to tell her that making off with a phone book was not exactly my idea of big-time crime. Instead I wrote down the number.

Thanks, I said, and pushed the book towards her.

Good luck, she said.

I looked at her and grinned. How did she know? For

a few moments I thought she could see right through me. I hated that. She could see my fear. I didn't like that. What if Carla was dead?

As I walked down the hall I wondered what the hell I was afraid of. I always feel uneasy about making a phone call and getting the wrong party. Sure I know I can hang up and no one will be the wiser. Yet when I hear a voice at the other end of the line that I don't know, I always get flustered and blurt out some silly apology, as if I've busted in on a couple making love. As if I've committed a crime. I know I've made the call. That's the point. And no matter what I do, no matter how I explain it to myself, or what I say to the person at the other end, if I dial a wrong number, I feel like I've made a damned fool out of myself. Annie says that's stupid. No one will remember, even if they know.

But I would, I say. I'd remember.

The phone had rung eight times.

Hello.

A woman answered.

Her voice paralyzed me. I wanted to hang up. I'd hoped Larry would answer. Chances were I'd recognize his voice. I couldn't remember what Carla's voice sounded like. Whoever the woman was she sounded tired. I'd probably wakened her.

Hello, she said again.

Is this the McCormack place? I asked.

I felt stupid. What did I expect? I'd just looked up

the number. But was it the right McCormack? And was this Carla?

I mean, I said, is this the L. J. McCormack who works in film and television?

Did, the voice said. Used to. Doesn't anymore.

The line went quiet. And then the voice spoke, the mouth a little closer to the phone.

Who is this, anyway?

Carla had always been feisty. This was a good sign.

Axel Sterne, I said.

Axel? I could hear her hesitate before she said, Axel, you asshole, it's ten thirty at night!

Carla?

Who were you expecting?

I don't know, I said. I don't know who I expected.

How was I supposed to tell her what I was thinking? I couldn't just say, So you're still alive, are you? Annie and I thought you might be dead. My free hand waved in the air as if I were batting away each silly thought that popped into my head.

What? she said.

Well, you know how it is these days? With marriage and all?

You and Annie still together? she asked.

Yes, I answered. I felt like I was cheating. I couldn't tell her about the packed bag I'd found in the closet of the spare room. How I'd gone down to the basement and punched a hole in the wall of my office. I couldn't speak of the ultimatums.

How is she?

Fine, I said. I wanted to tell her that Annie hadn't changed, hardly at all. That she still had the deep dimples when she smiled. And the same long blonde hair with bangs. I wanted to tell her that Annie still played opera on the stereo when she vacuumed and dusted. That she was as generous as ever. That she liked the Island, the isolation. That in spite of me she was at ease with her world.

Who would have thought, I heard her say. Jesus, Axel, we must be the only ones on the bloody planet who are still on our first marriages. She laughed. And it ain't from want of trying to leave, she said. God knows. Right?

I wondered what she meant. Was she referring to her illness? Or had she heard something about Annie and me? The road we'd travelled the last three years had been pretty rough.

So, what did you think? she asked again. Maybe you thought Larry might have found himself a younger woman? Or maybe you thought I was dead? Did you think I was dead, Axel?

I could hear her breathing at the other end of the line. She sounded asthmatic.

Did you?

No, I said quickly. No. None of those. I don't know what I thought. The lie seemed the wise way to go. Easier. I turned and looked through the bevelled glass of the entrance. Moonlight filtered through the tall firs and lit the rose garden with a blue glow. It was a cool light for such a warm summer evening. The pathway leading to the Tea House looked mysterious and forbidden.

How are you Carla? I asked.

I'm fine, Axel. Just fine, she said. Nice of you to ask. I get around as best I can. You know how it is? We get older. She laughed. Right?

She stopped talking. Then I heard her moving. I heard the rustle of cloth.

She said, I was lying down when you phoned.

Sorry, I said. You should have told me. I didn't mean to wake you. I guess I wasn't thinking. I didn't check the time.

You didn't wake me, she said. I'm glad you called. I still have to rest a lot. Sometimes I have to lie down for days on end. You know what it's like when you can't move? Nothing will stay still.

I could hear her laughing and wheezing at the other end of the line.

She said, Then I get this overwhelming urge to move. God I hunger to move. To run. Or, better still, fly. I'd like to walk in space. Do you know what I mean, Axel? Not to have to depend on anything or anyone for help? That's what I wish for when they tell me I have to rest. I want to move. Not lie here like I'm a goddamn corpse.

That doesn't sound so good, I said.

We all need our beauty rest, Axel. Some just need more than others. At least that's what they tell me. She laughed again. Her voice softened when she said, It's good to hear your voice, hon. How are you doing?

I'm all right, I said. What else could I say? I said, I'm

almost fifty. Remember when we used to joke that we'd be lucky if we made it to fifty?

Yes, she said. You were going to come to some dramatic end. In a racing car or at the top of some godforsaken mountain in the middle of the Alps. Good Christ, Axel, you used to get dizzy climbing a ladder.

This time when she laughed, she also snorted. Carla was enjoying herself at my expense. The sounds she made with her nose annoyed me.

I remember, I said, I remember. We were just kids. Give me a break. Anyway, unless I get hit by lightning, which seems about as likely as some quack writing me a prescription for whiskey, I'll be fifty in two months. Less a couple of days. But who's counting.

When I finished talking I could hear movement at the end of the line, but I sensed no one was listening. Carla, I said, you there? No one answered. Shit, I said. Carla, don't play games with me. Answer me, you hear? Larry? I pressed the phone into my ear until it hurt. Larry, you there? What's going on? Larry, answer me, I yelled. I turned to see the warden look out of her office down the hall towards me. She put a fat finger to her colourless lips and disappeared.

Part of me wanted to shout into the bitch's face. Up close. The other part of me was beginning to panic when I heard Carla say, Larry's asleep, Axel. It's late. We have separate rooms.

Where the fuck you been? I said.

I had to move, she said. Larry and I sleep apart so I won't wake him. My hours are quite irregular. And, as I told you, I need to move. I'm fine now. Besides, Larry has to go into the office in the morning.

What office? I asked. What's he doing these days?

The car dealership, she said. Didn't I say? She paused. Sorry, Axel, I thought I told you. Larry's a partner in a car dealership.

I thought only politicians owned car dealerships, I said. I knew as soon as I spoke I was going to say the wrong thing. Annie was always telling me I couldn't find a pair of feet large enough for my mouth. I tried to kill the snide tone but Carla picked up on it.

Cute, Axel, she said. Cute. Where you staying?

I twisted the phone cord around my fingers. I'm at the Redwood Centre, I said.

The detox place? Carla said. I could hear the surprise in her voice.

Not to worry, I said. I'm in the advanced stages of cure. I'm really here for the R&R. I wanted to joke about it but the jokes were all stale.

You're a boozer, Axel, she said. If you're staying at the Redwood Centre, you're a boozer. There is no cure, Axel. You just can't drink.

No, I said. I know that.

I wanted to tell her that I hadn't had a drink now for a month. At the beginning, the days blurred into one another a bit. I wanted to tell her about my mood swings. It was the mood swings I couldn't control.

Axel, she said, you need to talk to Larry.

Why is that? I asked. But I got the sense she was thinking of something else.

He can help you, she said. Believe me. He can help you, she said.

I wanted to ask her what special knowledge Larry had, but she said, I got to go Axel. It's late. I'll tell Larry you're here. He'll call and arrange to meet with you. I'd like to come along but I don't think they'll let me out. Not at the moment. She sounded breathless. Distant.

Carla, I said. But I heard the click at the other end of the line. Outside, the moon was half hidden behind a bank of cloud. The path was barely visible. Shadows moved like animals stalking the garden. For the first time in a long while I felt vulnerable. Afraid.

That had been two nights ago.

Since then I'd been to three sessions conducted by the warden, Mrs. Phyllis Staunton. She was tough, but I found I could open up to her. She didn't pry. She didn't nag or accuse. That's what I disliked the most. The accusations. With her I found myself talking, telling her things I'd never revealed to anyone else.

Annie and I always ended up screaming at each other. Insulting each other. Soon I was throwing things. Grabbing people. Hitting people I loved.

Phyllis said that was often the way we were. Men who drank. I'd be that way, she said, until I got the bug out of my brain. Nothing excused my behavior, she said, but it might help me to understand myself. To know that I was ill. I had to get rid of my guilt. This was the kind of shit I'd always figured was liberal double talk. Weakness mistaken for sickness. But I was at the point of revising that view.

When Larry phoned and asked me out to lunch, Phyllis went all soft at the mention of his name. This short, chunky woman who wore a grey wool suit on the hottest of summer days actually flushed in the cheeks when she heard the name of Larry McCormack.

Then she stammered that while normally contact with persons external to the programme was discouraged during the first week, of course I could have the afternoon off—that an afternoon with Mr. McCormack would do me a world of good. That there were few men as fine as Mr. McCormack.

And after all he has been through, she said.

The way she spoke, I thought I was going to lunch with a saint.

We have ordered lunch.

From the terrace I look out to the bay. Two sailboats ride at anchor. Larry hasn't said much since he gave me the tour of the dealership. I'm impressed. It's a sizeable operation. A lot of responsibility, I say, although I still find it hard to believe that anyone I know could be hawking cars for a living. I'd always thought of it as a profession for desperate men. He stares at me and I can only retreat to the bay and mountains beyond.

When I swing my head back, Larry is still studying me as if I'm a goddamn specimen on a slide. So I continue turning and look into the window at our reflection. Truth is, Larry looks a lot better than I do. He has a Latin complexion, a black beard which is peppered with just the right amount of grey, and a head full of silver hair. He's tall and has no gut to speak of. The tan slacks and blue-and-green checked sports shirt fit him as though a tailor's life had hung in the balance. He exudes confidence. Perfection. I feel anxious, keyed up, ready to spring. Then I see his lips move. I turn and look at the table in front of him.

You listening? he asks.

I nod.

Do you beat up on Annie? he says.

I want to protest. This is nuts. I didn't come out to lunch to be interrogated about my private life.

Do you? he insists. One thing I now remember about Larry is that he can be relentless.

Yes, I say. I mean, I used to. I haven't in a while, I say.

And the kids? he says. You do have kids?

Yes, I say.

Well? he says.

I give him a puzzled look. I want to divert his attention away from wherever he's taking us. When I look at him, his eyes give me the creeps.

Do you smack them around, too? he says.

I was crazy then, Lar. I didn't know what I was doing. I love them all, I say.

I'm about to crack. I can feel the tears in my eyes. I'm tempted to order a beer. I used to tell myself that one beer was not like an ounce of whiskey. I used to be able to divide my life up like that. Into parts.

I say, More often than not spanking them was a

matter of discipline. A way of keeping order in the household, I say.

Don't bullshit me, Axel, he says. Don't try to con someone who's been there.

We stare hard at each other. I want to tell him to get out of my face. He's beginning to smother me. There is an edge to his voice. My legs feel numb.

I turn away. I watch a gull swoop down and pull a shell out from between the rocks and barnacles.

After you moved, he says, after you moved, it took the doctors another two years to diagnose what was wrong with Carla. Her skin would turn and then heal. Turn and heal. They found out that her circulatory system hadn't developed properly. Blood wasn't getting to her hands and feet. Then the problem extended to her arms and legs.

The gull lifts off the ground, flies to thirty, maybe forty, feet.

He says, Then came the surgery. Four major surgeries on her nervous system. They needed to kill the signals being sent by the brain to the nerves that control the blood supply. Four major operations over two years. Three were relatively successful. She still needed to lie down, though. That's the only way her heart would pump blood to her whole body. And when she was lying down the pain subsided. But the fourth operation didn't work. Lesions kept appearing on her left arm. And they were growing larger and becoming infected.

The gull faces into the prevailing wind, glides and drops the shell. I hear the smack on the rocks, like a fist on flesh, and then watch the bird drop out of the sky to the beach, its beak pulling the guts out of the broken shell. I've always been squeamish. I want to tell him to stop. I've heard enough.

But he continues. The infection she has right now, he says, covers an area about this size. He uses his index finger to draw an imaginary line around his shoulder and down his chest. He traces back and forth over the line where Carla's breast would be.

Jesus Christ, Lar, I say. I had no idea.

She could die at any time, he says.

What confuses me is that I can hear no remorse, no distress in his voice. I'd be a basket case if it were Annie.

The sun pushes up above the trees. Soon we're feeling the full blast of the noonday heat.

How do you deal with it? I ask. Everything I'm thinking sounds trite.

Carla taught me. He pauses and folds his table napkin. Precisely, from corner to corner. We're dealt a hand, he says. Right?

I nod.

We can't change that hand, either. You understand? The timer's on.

That's a little too fatalistic for me, I say.

Don't be stupid, Axel. Listen to me. Listen carefully.

I want to run. Larry's mad. I want to tell him my fate is to run when I hear this kind of talk. But I'm stuck in my seat.

He says, After Carla's last operation I looked forward to see what my prospects were. I saw *nada*. Only a lot

of suffering. And I looked backwards to see if I could figure out what I'd done to deserve this. To love someone as
much as I do and then to have to watch her in this kind
of pain, well that was more than I could bear. So I drank.
I began and ended my days with gin. That was easy. Gin
was something, the one thing, I could count on.

What happened? I asked.

I quit, he says.

You quit, I say. Just like that! You quit. What am I
supposed to do, get down on my knees?

I live from day to day, he says. No magic.

Swell, I say. The breeze has picked up off the water. I
can feel the perspiration drying on my forehead. Is that
it? Is this all Phyllis's guru has to offer?

And Carla? I ask. What about Carla?

He smiles. Well, every so often, he says, I take a pillow and place it over her head. Usually in the morning, after coffee, just before I head off for work.

What? I say.

When I press down, he says, she wakes up. She
thrashes her legs and arms around a bit. Then in a
muffled voice, she says, That you, Lar? Honey, that you?
Yes, I say, yes it is dear. And she says, Tempted again are
you? Then we both laugh. A belly full of laughs, he
says.

You're sick, I say. This is morbid stuff, Lar. People are
committed for talking like this.

Then she tells me, not today. All right, Hon? Someday sweetie, she says to me. Someday. But please not
today, she always says.

He is on the verge of crying. Up in the trees the crows are talking to each other. I remember one day, when Annie and I arrived home, seeing two crows at the top of our driveway, one with its wing spread over the other.

Do you know what you're saying? I ask.

Yes, he says. Yes I do.

What? I say.

Love, he says.

But I can't figure if what he's said is a question or an answer.

The Plimsoll Line

Markers. We all have markers in our lives against which we measure our own failures and successes, I said to Henry. Markers against which we locate ourselves in time or, as is sometimes the case, deny our place in it, for there are occasions when we'd rather not find ourselves in the company of other men or women, when we feel embarrassed by the stories they tell and the events they celebrate. Some say they will always know what they were doing the day JFK was assassinated or remember the precise hour when Shepherd went walking on the moon, or, more recently, recall their first waking thoughts when they flicked on the news and watched scenes from the wedding of Charles and Diana. I said this one day a few years back when I was helping Henry dig post holes for the new fence he was building.

Henry said he hadn't much use for the monarchy. For royals of any sort.

That isn't my point, I said.

What *is* your point? he asked.

Only that recorded history is the selection of a few choice events, made arbitrarily by monks, court scribes, journalists or politicians, for example, to please those in power. And there are natural phenomena, I said, such as tornadoes, ice storms, floods, hurricanes, droughts, famines, that mark a year. That find their way onto the calendar of important events. They may do more to break up the monotony of time for most of us than reports of students rioting in Berkeley or Beijing. Or signify more than news flashes about the most recent crimes of the world's tyrants. Weather. That's what we remember from year to year. Crop failures. Poor fishing. Forest fires.

We washed our faces under the outdoor tap, and Hannah opened the screen door and passed out two gins and lemonade with ice.

We sat on the grass in the shade. I rolled my pants up to my knees to feel the breeze off the water cooling my legs.

Henry scrolled through those moments in his own lifetime that he said added up to nothing. Time wasted, he said. How does history account for that time? he asked. For most of it, as far as he was concerned.

When you write down what you know, Henry, that may be the most reliable historical record. To wait for events to conform to predictions or to confirm beliefs already held will most likely distort the commonest experience. Twelve long lifetimes pretty much take us back to the last turning of the millennium, I said.

Henry wiped his forehead with the palm of his hand, then reached over to one of the rose bushes and broke off a thorn which he used to clean under his thumbnail.

It's possible, I said, to know someone who knew someone who knew someone and so on who was in attendance at the birth of William the Conqueror. Mortality creeps up on us. There isn't that much distance between those who kept vestal virgins and us.

Perhaps, he said. But maybe history is what isn't said or recorded. Insert our dreams into the record and history is expanded infinitely. Breathe in one event daily, like the death of a boy, and time closes down on you. Sits on your shoulder and whispers in your ear. Hannah, on the other hand, he said, tallies up history with each beer she drinks.

For some, I said, there is only the moment.

Whistle a tune and I'll sing you my song, he said.

Something like that. History as vaudeville.

Fair enough. What do you call a five-hundred-year-old Irishman? he asked.

I don't know, I said.

Peat.

Now that's a marker, I said, to keep heart and hearth warm.

This is the story I want to tell.

Then he grabbed the boy, pulled him in close to his body and felt with his feet for the gravel bottom of the creek bed. But his legs shot out from under him, and he was swept along by the current. Fighting to regain control of his movements, he held the boy closer. Tighter. Embracing him. His water-filled boots and coat tugging him down.

This is what I scribbled into my notebook to remind me of important details when I came to write Henry and Hannah's story. I gaze out the window at the Lucas's house, my pen resting in my hand. I still make notes the old-fashioned way before I resort to the computer. I have a distrust of machines that move faster than the imagination. As it is, I remember more than I write down. My greatest fear is that I might take too many liberties with the facts. Their story springs from what we discussed, Henry and I, while standing next to the burn pile, throwing cuttings from the willows onto the bonfire. So if you wonder how I know as much as I do about Henry and his thoughts, remember that a warm fire, flames leaping into the air, embers burning like gold, can stir the most reluctant tongue. But Henry was easy, he liked to talk, to tell stories about his work in the woods amongst the giant firs.

And he had been in love.

Hooters, boobs, melons, he said.

You like women with large breasts? I asked.

I wouldn't tell you if I did. Some things are best left private.

And while warmth and the hypnotic effect of leaping flames are a catalyst for the truth, so, too, is beer. I have recollections of what Hannah said on the many evenings we spent drinking together in the village pub. A few pints, blended with the singing voices of companions, soon command their own obedience to a version of reality that is difficult to dispute.

The house is empty now, awaiting new occupants, hopefully a young family. Someone to use the rope swing Henry tied to an arm of the willow. Someone to putter in the kitchen in which Hannah put up preserves—peaches, plums, cherries, pears, and pickles.

In April, when the spring run-off from the snowmelt back on the hills behind the village streamed together with heavy rains, and Knarston Creek swelled and spilled over its banks into back yards and flooded paths and roadways, Henry Lucas, out for his morning walk, saw a small boy lean through the lower railings of one of the bridges and fall, in a blink of Henry's eyes, into the creek's turbulent surge. The boy was gone quickly, out of sight. Then Henry saw him shoot to the surface, his arms clutching at the air. Henry ran along the bank, caught up to him and jumped in, grabbed the boy, pulled him close to his body and felt with his feet for the gravel bottom of the creek bed. When his legs shot out from under him, when he felt the current pull him down, he gripped the boy tighter, held on to him so fiercely that he could feel the boy's neck give way, softly, in his arms. He had panicked at a time when everyone was always commenting on how reliable he was. How sure-footed. Henry Lucas could be counted on. He was trustworthy. Yet he had strangled the boy. Suffocated him. So easily. Henry didn't know his own strength.

Never had. Always so close to violence, even in an act of mercy.

I'm concerned that I be precise, so I deliberately attempt to avoid any embellishments that might suggest judgement, however impractical that might be. Stories by their nature reveal decisions and consequences, but in this case let those be Henry's and Hannah's.

I can't remember the year I first saw them, but it must have been shortly after I moved to the village. They were already old, at least to my eyes, especially him, bent over, his skin so white, with brown pigment splotches, his back humped, grey hairs growing out of his nose and ears. Hannah diverted attention away from herself with the stories she told, with her bird-like voice, singing. She didn't want anyone to notice how difficult movement had become, how shapeless she had become. Arid. Dry as a desert coulee.

We never had children, Henry said, so you will have to do. You will be our memory.

We sat around a table covered with glasses of beer.

You remembering the boy? Hannah asked.

Right away she realized she shouldn't have said anything, but Henry had that look on his face, that look of surprise he got when he couldn't quite comprehend his place in a world that allowed murderers, like him, to walk about freely. The words the coroner had used, accidental manslaughter, had not eased his conscience. He told us that in his dreams he saw the small face turn white, the mouth slacken, wordless beneath the cold, green water.

I am.
You shouldn't
I know.
Henry shook his head and examined his glass with great thoughtfulness. And you shouldn't drink so much beer, he said.
In a pig's eye!
Don't flatter yourself.

Hannah Lucas lifted her glass and looked at it closely. She wanted to be certain that when the head of foam settled she would get her legal limit of beer. Ever since the government had insisted on inscribing all beer glasses with a white line half an inch from the rim, and a few months later under threat from publicans had removed the mark, she figured Abel Tilliard had tried every trick in the book to cheat his customers. Hannah knew that a larger head meant less beer. And more gas. And Hannah loved her beer. Without gas.

So Henry had to wait before he drank. Hannah insisted. When Robbie Robertson proposed a toast, Henry sat perfectly still and studied his glass with an intensity that might have been mistaken by someone from outside the village for thoughtful meditation rather than the obedience we knew it to be. Then his sad old sea-lion eyes glanced down to his right hand. His fingers, splayed awkwardly at the burled knuckles, lay motionless and crippled on the table. Whatever life had once flowed through those hands had long ago drained into the earth. After a short while the gnarled fingers moved slowly across the table to wrap themselves around the bottom of the glass. As Hannah watched Henry she wondered how she had ever allowed those hands to touch her, to cup her breasts. She struggled to recall the process, to sift out the correct images, but memory presented itself in generalities. She wanted to slip back, recollect specific details, rather than rely on the reflections she stole from observing young families growing up around her. Second and third growth she wanted to yell at them. But those hands, his hands, kept intruding.

Age is in the hands, she said. You can always tell how worn down a person is by their hands. Don't look at their faces, faces can mask age. A few wrinkles are more than likely a consequence of habit, not a sign of age. No, the hands are key. Pinch the flesh, like this, and she caught the back of Henry's hand between her thumb and forefinger, and watch how the flesh regains its shape. Elasticity. If the skin doesn't snap back, then the person has aged. Beyond their years. Unless they're old, of course, like Henry.

Disgust flushed quickly across Hannah's face, visible even in the dim afternoon light of the bar, and Henry's hand withdrew over the edge of the table and disappeared into his lap.

He was trying to save the boy, he told us. He was trying to save him, Henry told everyone, as if they didn't believe him. But the creek was too deep, deeper than he expected, the rush of water so swift, he lost control of his footing. And the young neck, fragile, had given way, collapsed, in the crook of his arm.

As they wrapped blankets around him to warm him, as he gazed down on the body of the young boy at his feet, Henry wept. He didn't know his own strength.

If we could change places, he said to those who watched him. If only, he said, as if they could make it possible.

He felt a hand pat him on the shoulder.

Fuck it, he said, fuck it all anyway, and he turned and walked away from the police, the firemen, the neighbours who had gathered at the creek's edge near the bridge he'd used to lever himself out of the water.

In my notebook I have written: Providence is sometimes an unlucky charm. I can't remember the source of this observation. And is it true? Below, on the same page, I have noted that an abundance of weeds, grass and a few wild poppies, as orange as the sun on a late summer night, have overgrown the ashes where the burn pile danced above the earth.

Henry waited to drink.

After the Plimsoll Line appeared, a line Hannah continued to store in her memory, the amount of draught pulled from the tap hadn't changed, but the price had increased steadily from twenty-five to thirty to thirty-five to forty cents. And with no limit in sight. When the price broke the dollar barrier, she said it was a shame such things were allowed to happen.

She pursed her lips and squinted as if there were a bright light shining in her eyes.

Before that both she and Henry could remember a

time when a full glass of beer was ten cents. Yet neither could recall exactly what the price had been way back, before the Winnipeg Strike of 1919 and, later, the crash of '29. All that remained in their minds were the headlines which reported mounted police riding into crowds, men trampled under hoof. The riots and blood-wash blotting out details from their own past. Then, even more fantastic and commonplace in its recurrence, came news of bodies launching into flight from the tallest buildings in New York city, swan songs to the hard reality of pavement. This event had all but erased memory of their early years together.

And so, perhaps the price of beer had once been as much as it was now, Hannah suggested. Who was to know if the two of them couldn't dredge up the very silt of their own experience. Their own memories, like the earth itself, victims of time. Of the flow of ice-caps and oceans which buried whole civilizations, whole continents beneath a moraine of new shapes. At times, Hannah said, memory was little more than a voice fired in anger from the belly of the earth.

Memory is hell, she said.

Henry stared at her, as if trying to bring her words into focus.

That's right, Henry! Not flames licking at our legs like we're told, but memories. What we remember. With each breath, that's what burns in our hearts.

And then we're dead, Henry said to Hannah one day, out of the blue. Suddenly dead. One minute you're looking out the kitchen window at the seabirds along the shore, gulls and mergansers, buffleheads and surf scoters, and the next minute you're dead, unseeing, unfeeling, untasting, unthinking, unconscious. Unhealthy, for sure. People complain about built-in obsolescence, but it's everywhere, built into the very core of being. Burnout! Rust! Wear and tear. He looked at Hannah and said, You look awful. She was not the woman he had married. Not at all. No matter what she did to slow down the decay.

Hannah knew Henry was right. She no longer cared for herself as she had in the past. No eyeliner, mascara, or rouge. Her hair was unbrushed, a chaos of curls and tangles. She no longer used perfumes, fragrances guaranteed to induce longing and desire. What would be the point!

And Henry was certainly not one to talk. Her eyes lingered on the grey stubble of his caving cheeks, pouches left by lost teeth. Poor Henry. Poor sweet old Henry. Good God, what a fool; what an ineffectual old fool. Without dignity only pity was possible. This end, this culmination of the whole absurd kaleidoscoping narrative of their lives revolted her.

After such a long wait, Hannah knew the beer would be flat and warm.

Rain fell against the window and each newly formed drop ran its course down the glass before disappearing without a trace. She felt betrayed and degraded. She watched the last of the foam slide toward the line.

Both pensions combined were hardly enough to keep

pace with the crazy, maddening increase in the cost of everything that made their old age even slightly bearable. There was no justice.

Inflation. Everything was blamed on this mysterious word 'inflation'. She was certain there were people somewhere who were paid enormous salaries to invent words, sayings, slogans to baffle, hypnotize the public, bury whatever horrible truth was in store for them all. None of the talk on the radio, nor what she read in the newspapers, made the least bit of sense. Increased labour costs. Decreased production. Devaluation of the Pound Sterling. Arab oil dollars. The German Mark. Contract negotiations. Strategic arms talks. *Détente*. Economic sanctions. What did these words have to do with her or Henry? She agreed with the hotliners though. It was the old-age pensioners, those on fixed incomes, people like her and Henry, they were the ones suffering the most at the hands of this word inflation. If they weren't reduced to eating dog food now, as one angry hotliner said was happening to many pensioners, she was positive they'd be reduced to such humility soon enough. Fixed incomes! She and Henry knew precisely what that meant.

Henry made her angry at times. He paid little or no attention to the radio, and most often dropped off into a light sleep a few minutes after her favourite hotline programme began.

How are we to know, Henry? she asked. Tell me that. How are we to know what's going to happen to us? Henry? Listen to me!

Nothing, absolutely nothing penetrated that thick

balding skull of his. His lack of interest annoyed her most. His sleeping, even his sleeping, was preferable to that contemptuous flick of his hand. Normally he snored his way through the phone calls and then miraculously woke up the moment she shut off the radio.

Was there anything new? Had anything new happened? he asked.

Anything new happened! she said. Damn it, Henry. Just listen for once. Listen for God's sake.

Doesn't seem to me anything new ever happens, he said.

How in hell would you know, you're never awake. Stay awake for a few minutes and you'd know the whole damn world is going to waste, to ruin. Nothing, nothing makes sense any more. Nothing, she would emphasize.

That so?

That's right.

Why do you bother to listen then? If it don't make sense.

Because I have to. One of us has to. I want to understand, Henry. I want to know . . .

What? Want to know what?

What's in store for us for Christ's sake.

He shook his head.

No rest, he said, makes for a long, unhappy life.

Not you though, she answered back. You could give a damn. For you the future is a blank canvas. You've given up on hope. For years it was trees. Now it's nothing but fishing. Abel could charge you full price for half a glass of beer and you'd just sit there and accommodate him.

A bird in the hand, Henry said and smiled.

Hannah looked around the beer parlour. Nothing had changed its appearance, not even the yearly layer of diluted paint, a sickly combination of pale green and salmon, that Abel Tilliard rolled onto the walls each year on the Sunday before Labour Day. She wondered if anyone else saw a deliberate irony in this gesture. He's a wicked man, she said, living off the pleasures and vices of others as he does. Then she gave a grunt, clearing her throat, and licked her lips.

She watched the faces of her friends, each smeared with heavy layers of cosmetics. Each blown figure, her own as much as the others, distended and threadbare. How had they changed? The passing of thirty years was barely perceptible to that slow movement of eyes. A regular house of mirrors, like she had seen at the Pacific National Exhibition years earlier, where figures were distorted and grotesque. Laughable. Now, her own dress, she recalled out of the morning mirror, hung about her shapeless body like sackcloth, making her look more and more like a lumpy bag of potatoes. The 'sweet violets' of the print faded past mourning. No lace, no frills could disguise the habit of her dress. Only when she recognized Dick Spicer sitting alone in the furthermost corner of the room, without Alice, did she realize how sudden and swift change could be. Poor Alice, an incurable romantic, had been a stocky one hundred and eighty pounds one day, and a wisp of a thing picked up and whisked away on the wind the next day. Or so it seemed.

Right then, right at that moment, she wanted to scream out at Henry: Don't you see what's happening? What chance have we got? Have we ever had? Listen to me, Henry! God damn it all to hell, listen. Open your eyes.

The years spent in the woods had silenced his youthful anger, the ardour she remembered from those first few years of their marriage. In those early days, when he returned home from the camp, he stomped about the house in his calkboots, leaving long scuff marks and scratches in the linoleum. Before he was able to make love to her, he spent days circling within the house, yelling past her, out through the kitchen window toward the sea as though the sea were the only place large and impersonal enough to cast his thoughts. He yelled about the asinine management, about conditions in the camp, and swore that he'd never return to that hellhole. She was quick back then to learn patience.

For a week, sometimes more, he carried on this ritual, hardly aware of her presence, until finally the late autumn motion of the sea and the rhythms of her body moved in to possess his thoughts. One day he cautiously took her hand in his and pressed so tight she feared the small bones in her fingers might be crushed. Pleased by this first gesture of desire she became acutely conscious of her own attractiveness. She longed to control the uncertainty of his moods. This island, she said, averting her face to the sea so he wouldn't notice her tears, has a curious way of separating.

Suddenly, daring himself into an awkward boldness, he wrapped his arm around her waist, encircling her like the high wooded cliffs encircled the secluded bay by which they walked. His hands, covered with cuts and calluses, were rough and painful to her young breasts. She feared his strength but as his arm moved up her back she allowed his power to pull her, like the incoming tide, into the shell of his warmth. After silent walks along the beach, the crash of late October waves over the rocks began to purge his anger. And soon her intimate scent and the smell left by the shifting tides replaced the smell of moss and rotting undergrowth and the stench of the bunkhouse.

At first he bathed twice a day, while she picked lice from his hair. Then she soaped and scrubbed his scalp with her fingertips until she heard him sigh, until she felt his pleasure ripple through her body. Yet, when he finally crawled into her bed, he still worried about his being too close. And when she teased him with her newly painted nails, he withdrew further into himself, to a place where no one could follow. It was as though he feared he carried the camp on his body, like a contagious disease that would infect her.

Every year in the woods there were accidents and Henry told the stories. Sometimes it was fire or a freak storm and wash, but more often than not it was the equipment. Lousy, cheap bloody gear, he said. The bosses don't give a shit about us. All that matters to those bastards is how many trees we knock down in so many goddamn hours. Board feet, he said angrily, board feet's all that concerns them. Hire kids who've never seen a tree felled and expect 'em to learn on the job.

As he spoke I could smell sawdust and moss, the dampness of the soil beneath the undergrowth.

Henry said he turned when he heard two men shouting, the two men pulling on the Swede saw. He turned in time to see the Douglas fir stutter step to the right, like it was about to dance the tango, and then plunge forward, the butt end kicking backwards, towards the third man who stood directly behind. Who seemed stuck to the spot, as if his feet had been nailed down. Who couldn't dance because he didn't know the steps. Didn't know which way to move. How to move. Henry said he cried out to warn him, but the tree kicked back, the butt end striking upwards. Catching the man totally unawares, lifting his head clean off his shoulders.

Murder, Henry said softly. It was murder.

For sixty cents a day, for Christ's sake.

Only this man was not a man, he was a boy, no more than sixteen. Barely shaving. First day on the job. The kid was put on a three-man falling crew. As oiler. To lubricate the saw while the other two cut. But the two men pulling on the saw didn't know what they were doing. Didn't get the lean right. Didn't make the proper undercut.

The tree, not the saw, kicked back.

When they propped the kid up against a stump, sat him there as if he were at peace with all wild things, to wait for someone to take him out, the two men repeated, over and over, that they were sorry. They tried as best they could to set his head back on his shoulders. To make this head—jaw crushed, nose buried in his skull, eyes swollen—look like it belonged. As if the thing torn apart were a stuffed doll that could be sewn back together again.

When the accident whistle blew down the line, when the wives and girlfriends gathered at the railway station, all in a panic, no one was there to answer the call. The kid had no one. Not even family.

For sixty cents a day.

That's murder, clear enough, Henry said. Murder.

After a week, two at the most—some years were worse than others—he'd roll over in the night and take her into his arms. It was then she could feel the energy rush from his fingers. A rush rich with life, like the explosive burst of green in spring, at a time when the world outside lay under the first light moonlit cover of snow. Back in the mountains the camps and equipment rested dead and forgotten under piling drifts.

Henry caressed her hair, brushed it back off her face, then quickly kissed her. His fingers scarcely touched her and yet he could feel her tremble, like alder leaves, a light flutter in the wind. He could feel her muscles grow taut, feel her restraint, as if she were attempting to control the movement of air. Each breath she took. Later, as they lay in bed, he almost pulling and squeezing her from the very roots of her own being, he tasted tears rolling off her cheeks and into his mouth. That same night he would draw away, his body tense to her touch.

The following morning he sat and gazed out past the small orchard at the sea, the islands, the snow-capped mountains on the mainland. Not once did he look her way. She was puzzled over this initial reaction of his to their first intimacy after a long spring and summer apart. If it were shame he felt, she was unable to understand it. She longed to understand but feared even more his stubbornness. God but he could be stubborn! Was she at fault? To blame? And for what exactly?

She hadn't the courage to ask what troubled him and retired to the kitchen where she busied herself putting up the last of the preserves. She never spoke to him about her own longing, never told him how during his absence her nipples grew tender to touch, how on hot summer evenings she rubbed her whole body with lavender oil. She never told him how she dug and turned the earth in the vegetable garden until every leg, arm and back muscle hurt, hurt so much she no longer felt her own ache for sex. She never revealed to him how late at night, in the lingering glow of a sunset, she lay in bed listening to the angry slaps and forlorn cries of old bulls left behind by the herds of sea lions who had spent the winter camped on the islands at the entrance to the bay.

That afternoon, he put on his hat and mackinaw and struck out down the hill toward the beach where he walked for miles. It was evening before he returned. His cheeks were flushed and his breathing was heavy with exertion. Whatever had bothered him earlier was now resolved in his own mind, and his eyes, which for the first week or two had barely been able to contain a wildness within, were now composed, now looked into her eyes with a sureness and ease. He closed the bedroom curtains and motioned for her to join him in bed.

But when he fell asleep he began to moan, a voice rising from deep inside, from another time and place, a grieving. She knew he was remembering the boy. Henry held her, one hand placed tentatively in the small of her back, the other tangled in her hair, and she listened to his keening song, and whispered, What happened to the boy was a mistake. An accident. If you hadn't jumped into the creek after him he would have drowned anyway. Do you understand that, Henry? You want to be forgiven for what everyone but you knows was a terrible accident.

When winds out of the northwest busted open the cloud-grey sky and frost was driven from the soil, brant returned to the bay on their migration back to nesting grounds in the Arctic tundra. When the winter weather finally broke, when the heavy snows back on the mountains began to melt, Henry's face, which had grown pallid and a bit fleshy from the lazy days indoors, showed, like the seasons themselves, signs of being restless. He forgot to shave and to cut his fingernails. Anxiety spread through his entire body. He grew fidgety at the supper table and whenever he sat his right leg began to bounce up and down involuntarily. And then, one day, every year was the same, he jumped out of his large stuffed chair in the living room, walked out of the house, past the tool-shed, and made his way down the rockery to the two large weeping willows in the front yard. Still wearing his slippers and still in shirt-sleeves, he climbed into the trees and began sawing and clipping off branches. Two hours later he returned to the house and began to pack his gear. He grumbled that it was a hell of a way for a man to earn his living, but it was the only way he knew how. Those damn trees were in his blood.

To listen to Henry, he'd been climbing around and up trees before he'd been able to utter a word. Even with arthritis bending his back, he volunteered to help his neighbours top trees that blocked their views of the sea. And every time his broken fingers tied on the old boots, dug out the ropes and those huge deformed hands tugged the chain saw into life, he winced. The pain rolled around inside his head, travelled out to and back from all the bones he'd broken. When Hannah complained he was too old, he'd point to the chain saw he'd bought a couple years back and say, That makes her easy. Child's play. Too easy, he'd say.

At these moments I remember his eyes, how wild they were. Whether with loss, anticipation, anger, or fear, I cannot say. Otherwise, he was a model of perfect emo-tional control.

Henry looked at Hannah who watched him from across the table. He could read her thoughts. Nothing was hidden anymore. After sixty-two years, he could feel her disgust, his old body almost more than her love could bear, like an old coat that's grown too comfortable to discard but, all the same, looks like hell.

During the thirties life in the camps had become unbearable. Everyone who was in a position to do so took advantage of the Depression. Henry and a few others from the village who worked the same camp had complained in writing to management in Vancouver about the conditions throughout the whole operation. They had even gone so far as to make suggestions on how matters could be improved. They had all signed their names to a petition. Soon after that a few of them tried to organize into a union and the companies had responded by firing every last one of them and blacklisting them with other companies from one end of the island to the other. Henry insisted he'd never work another camp, but a few months later a small operation back in the Cowichan Valley hired on all those who had been blacklisted. The best loggers on the island had ended up in that camp. Most of them had remained there until certification in '37. Even so, Hannah had told them they should dynamite the camps of the larger companies, had even encouraged them to sabotage the sons-of-bitches. But Henry would have none of her talk. He figured by firing them the damage had already been done.

Who's left to knock down their damn trees, he said.

Henry had taught Hannah to sing from her heart, to love song as if it were what charged the surge of blood through the body. He taught her to play a tune on the upright piano using only the black notes. He showed her how to smoke salmon with dry alder wood in a converted refrigerator. He showed her how to chop wood, how to sharpen an ax so it cut through wood like a knife through the soft flesh of an apricot. He told her that while he loved the crevices and curves of her body, all the secret places she willed him to discover, she should have been a man with her temper. Henry, who had once been as straight, as tall, as strong as any of the godforsaken trees he'd cut out of the forest, this man whose bowed head held such ridiculous dreams, was now little more than a wreck of a thing. They had no right, no right at all, to take his life from her.

For fifty-six years, from the time he was fifteen, Henry worked in the bush. As Hannah looked around the beer parlour she realized most of the men had been in logging. Few of them looked even as good as Henry. Now, like him, most of them spent their early mornings out fishing. One day, she figured, those who had survived logging would perish at sea. That would be the final irony. Although they had learned to watch every move in the woods, treat every move as a potential source of death, in their small fishing boats they played like reckless children. At sea there was no possibility of a tree falling, no risk, they seemed to feel, of the unpredictable. As near as she could figure, each salmon or cod caught was Henry's solution to all their problems.

There's more than enough for all of us in the sea, he'd say. And besides, there's always the garden, Hannah, don't forget the garden.

That's right, she'd answer, that's right, Henry. And if someone told you to stand on your head and piss in your pockets, you'd try to oblige them.

Henry had opened his mouth to respond, but stopped and closed his eyes. Once again he'd shut himself off from the light of the world. You're becoming soft, she said, like the flesh of an artichoke.

Hannah looked out the window, past the railing and posts that held up the false front of the white- and blue-trimmed hotel, at the grey sky and sea. Can't tell where one meets the other, she muttered. Can't even see the nearer islands, let alone the mainland. Rain, she said, this place is miserable with rain. Comes at you from all sides, above and below. And when it splashes off the pavement up your skirt, you feel like you're walking in the sky.

She had insisted they sit by the window. She liked to watch the new houses being built on the old site of the mining camp. A year ago they had bulldozed down the old bunkhouses. An eyesore some had claimed. And now they were raising brand new luxury homes. How people afforded such mansions she couldn't fathom. At least she and Henry owned their own place, small and run down as it was. Henry had promised to do some painting as soon as it came summer.

She watched Henry, who was saying something to Sammy Darling about fishing. How they were going to paint the place and continue eating she simply couldn't figure. Not with the cost of things these days.

Don't give me none of that bullshit about the good

old days, Henry had said. We ain't never had it so good. No siree! We'll find a way, don't you worry.

His certainty pleased him.

Good, she said. Good! You're an old fool Henry Lucas, a damn fool. You've no idea how much it costs to live these days. You probably still think hens lay eggs, that cows give milk, that potatoes grow in hills of soil. It's all done by science now. Hydroponics. We live like tadpoles. I've seen it on TV.

She began to laugh but phlegm got caught in her throat. There was nowhere to spit so she searched her pockets for a handkerchief.

That was it. He'd say no more. Apart from talk about fishing, a topic he could speak on for hours, he lacked opinions of any sort on any subject. Even when they brought in an old-age pension scheme for loggers, one year after his retirement, and he found out he wasn't eligible after one trip down to the Union Hall, he just resigned himself to the fact. After fifty-six years, after fighting all those years for the union, he wasn't even prepared to fight for what she felt was his rightful due. And all she had wanted was enough money for a table full of cold beer. Enough to feel the pressure against her bladder just one last time.

I've had it with logging, he said. Besides, the government pension'll do us fine. He steadied his voice and shook his head. We'll manage.

How? Hannah had asked.

All the froth had disappeared off the beer and to

Hannah's disappointment the measure in both hers and Henry's glasses fell right on the mark. She looked towards the bar where Abel stood smiling back at her. Damn his hide anyway, she thought. The man was a pig. If she thought could get away with it, she would have sipped a bit off the top and then complained, but Abel watched her with those small crow eyes of his, watched for her to take that first sip.

There was a time, she said, when you could judge a good beer parlour by how damp the table top was from beer spilling over the side and down the glass.

Now, she reflected, the only moisture on the glass was condensation.

She nodded to Henry who waited patiently for her to give him permission to drink. At first he had complained that waiting caused the beer to go flat, but she always insisted they wait to see that Abel had properly filled the glasses.

What's the time? Henry asked quite suddenly.

Ten past three, she said.

Every day they came to the beer parlour at exactly the same hour and every day Henry wanted to know the time. Why he cared what hour it was he wouldn't say. She worried that he was finally going senile. That whatever brain cells he'd had, had up and carried out their own funeral inside that bony casket of a head.

What?

Ten past three! Why don't you listen? Listen for Christ's sake!

Juke box. Can't hear for the music.

Hannah tapped her glass with her fingernail, making a sound like a metronome. Time's so short, she said. Time passes so quickly, Henry, when you're reminded of it. When you get old.

It's not time that's the problem, he said. It's life. Life's too short.

One hardly has any meaning without the other, as far as I can see.

When God made time, Henry said, He made plenty of it.

That's silly! Who's to know? Sometimes you're too gullible Henry. Keeping track, that's the problem. Always wanting to know where we are in time. That's the lie of it. Where we are in time. Are we near the beginning or near the end? How can we know?

Henry shrugged and removed the glasses he wore when he was trying to see things up close.

We can't know, Hannah said. That's the point. When does time stop and when does it start? She stared up at the ceiling, her eyes empty and sad. When I was a little girl and asked my mother how old she was, she would say, The same age as my tongue and a little older than my teeth.

Henry grinned, showing the gaps in his mouth.

I get it, Hannah said. I wasn't born yesterday.

You can say that again, Henry said, and slid his hand across the table towards her. He gave a little chuckle. Doesn't matter, though. Hasn't mattered in years. He leaned towards her. Nothing's easy, Hannah, nothing. We all want to go back and make things different. Recover something we've lost. He took in a deep breath. But maybe we don't lose things, we give them up. Or let someone take them from us. Maybe men die younger because they give up first. Happiness has nothing to do with age.

She watched him closely to see if he were trying to trick her.

It's the thought of being alone that I fear the most, she said.

The voice of Willie Nelson sang from the speakers hidden in corners around the room.

Hannah and Henry sipped their beer. They could no longer afford to drink quickly. She felt embarrassed and humiliated; old age hardly seemed reason enough for sobriety. Quite the reverse.

It had been too long since either had awoken the next morning with a head that paid tribute to the evening before. Hannah took another sip from her glass and watched the carpenter across the way framing one of the new homes. It had started to rain and the early winter sky darkened. Everything was turning grey or black. Even the trees appeared black without sunlight. Sometimes, during the winter, she felt submerged, as though she were living underwater.

What's the time? Henry asked again.

Five minutes later than when you asked the first time, she said, looking at her watch.

No doubt about it, his mind was going. The past five minutes had already sifted below the layer of recall.

Where'd you get the watch?

Alberni, she said. My God, she thought, either he was making conversation or his mind had finally deserted him.

You gave it to me. For my birthday. Remember? she tested.

He paused. His words had nothing to do with what they were saying. They were searching for another moment, another event.

Uh huh! Alberni. That would have been in Alberni. When I was working for M&B. When we was up there for three years, wasn't it?

Five, she said

Five? Five, that's right. For five years. Didn't like living there. Away from here. Away from home. When did we leave there then? Come back here? Must be nineteen, twenty years now.

Twenty-four! It was twenty-four years ago! she said.

Hannah could feel the blood pounding through her temples. Henry barely moved when the flat of her hand hit the table top. She was surprised by the swiftness of her action. And embarrassed. There had to be a reason. An explanation. He was becoming impossible. And with nothing to discuss but a past he barely remembered.

Twenty-four years! Imagine that, twenty-four years! You sure?

She hesitated. She hated this. His body gone, she wasn't sure she could abide his senility, if that was what it was. He didn't seem to care anymore. The constant worry that they might have to sell the house, that they wouldn't be able to pay the taxes, persisted in her mind. But Henry didn't care. He'd lost all contact. And now his memory. She wasn't sure she could make it on her own. Care for the place and him both.

Yes, I'm sure. That was the year William moved to Vancouver.

Henry lifted the glass to his lips and slowly drank off his beer. A white film formed an ugly, splotchy pattern on the inside of the glass.

Well, well, he said. Imagine that. Twenty-four years. Time sure do fly, don't it?

Angrily Hannah raised her arm, about to finish off what remained in her glass, but catching sight of Abel smiling down toward the two of them she replaced the glass on the table with just half an inch of tepid beer left in the bottom.

So I've told their story. Many of the details important to the lives of Henry and Hannah are common to any older couple living in this village, where most of the men fished or logged to earn a living and most of the women stayed at home to raise children. A few kept goats and chickens, and tended small kitchen gardens. There would be nothing remarkable in all of this if we still had trees and fish to harvest—and I'm not one to suggest that we'd be any happier for what we've lost, but I do know the roads and shops would not be deserted and our children would not have to be bussed over twenty kilometres into the city for schooling. As I say, there are these markers stretching out before us and behind us, linking us with who we were and who we hope to become, a song of sorrow for all we've known and hope to know.

No matter what anyone says, Hannah said, for my money Henry was hung like a bull.

Water and time. Henry hadn't understood the power of water, the force it gained rushing headlong between banks. Searching. Pushing everything in its path. The boy's neck had given way in the V of his arm just before he reached the bridge, just before he managed to grab a brace with his free hand, flesh scraping away from his wrist to his elbow, the force of the surging water almost pulling his arm from its socket, his fingers aching, digging into the wood. His feet propelled towards the surface, his boots banging against a piling. In one motion he heaved the boy upwards, like a sack of flour, pliant. Then he levered himself up onto the bridge deck. There he sat, trying to catch his breath— time collapsed, moving neither forward nor backwards—looking down at the boy's face, so pale, his body, so limp. Time swirling below in a black rage.

He couldn't forget.

When Henry grew too feeble to walk the half kilometre to the pub and appeared to lose all interest in his garden, Hannah insisted they move to an apartment in the city only a few kilometres away. You'll be able to come back and visit whenever you want, she said. But once they'd settled into what Henry called the mortuary, boxes inside of boxes, the air artificial and sweet, he never stirred from the large wingbacked chair where he sat staring out past the balcony at the small islands in the harbour.

On the one occasion when I had the opportunity to visit with them, he asked after the boy. Hannah looked at Henry, then at me, her face at once stern and pleading, and said, The boy is fine, dear, the boy'll be just fine.

A few weeks later, when she came in from shopping, she found Henry slumped over, his chin resting on his chest. She took the blanket crumpled at his feet and spread it over his legs and lap, and tucked the edges under the cushion. You need to keep yourself warm. Taking his hand, she said, You're chilled. How many times do I have to tell you? Keep yourself warm.

She wasn't sure why she did this, she told me. Panic, perhaps. Then she stepped back to look at him. Why? she said, why oh why? You were never as strong as you thought, she said to him.

Before she reached the phone, she told me softly, almost apologetically, before she made the call, she fell to her knees and closed her eyes. As if trying not to see what she knew was there. He was my only lover. I shouldn't be telling you this. Everything was done in the dark in those days. As if we were afraid of our own flesh. Once he got rid of the camp smell, he was good to me, she said. Gentle and kind. We led such sheltered lives.

As we talked and strolled through the park after the funeral, she hooked her hand around my arm, glanced up at me, her grey eyes imploring, and asked, The boy—she paused and cleared her throat—he'll be okay, won't he?

Her fingers, bird-small and yellowed by nicotine, barely made an impression through the cloth of my coat.

Yes, I said, and nodded, he'll be okay. He'll be just fine.

Feathering To Infinity

When the carpenter set his square into corners and took measurements from the recently bared studs and joists, he found the floor in our home bowed and warped in every direction. Nothing was level or straight. The entrance hall sloped at least four inches to the south and had been built in a different season, on a day when rainfall transcended indifference. I can feather the floor out to infinity, he said, and he began to cut pieces of plywood, shaped into huge wedges of pearled pine, and placed one on top of another to raise one corner to the level of the others. He took a reading from his compass, tapped the barometer, and moved slowly outward, toward the horizon. As he grew smaller and we feared he'd reach infinity, we told him he'd best return. You're one heart beat from vertical, we yelled, from where the lark's song spills into nightfall. We'll learn to live with the slope in the floor, I pleaded. Bow, my wife corrected. We'll learn to adapt, I said. We'll learn to walk with one leg shorter than the other, she said. Better that than lose a fine artisan. Not to mention a friend, she added.

On the last day we saw him, he was a speck on the earth's cusp, our floor as flat as an oak table top, a slice of marble, an open sea, or a ploughed field naked under a prairie sky.

Neither of us has remarked on the incline in years, nor can we recall how it was before. Before the spiders left the comfort of their nests. Before their cobwebs were torn and the sun broke through windows as if through the spokes of a wheel. Each spring, we quarrel about which corner the potted fern slipped into before our world became perfectly flat. But the carpenter is more than a memory, for it was he who brought proportion into our lives and made us see the beauty of figures and words woven in the wrist.

Shade

Some men grow old gracefully and probably go to heaven, God bless their souls, while others are ground down until only the pip is left, something to plant, to grow anew, a replenishing of the soil, if there's enough rain, ample drainage, sunlight, no hardpan, the pH is right, and there aren't too many stones to pick up. Too much of any one of these can break a man's back or break his will. No amount of plotting or prayer by us is going to alter this course of events. But when your own neighbours or the government conspire against you, well, that's another matter.

Then all men, no matter what their occupation, grow weary.

This was the substance of our conversation after Abel's funeral service at the Anglican church. We were all sitting around tables at the Legion. Family included. I was relieved it wasn't the hotel. No doubt about it, there was criticism implicit in what was said. Blame raised its ugly head and everyone felt uncomfortable. In fact, I'm told that later that night a fistfight broke out between a couple of long-time friends.

For my part, I wanted to be alone, not because I was his wife and felt I should bear my sorrow in solitude, but because I could see him more clearly while alone. Like Emily in her paintings, I've always been able to tunnel into the forest and leave the bickering behind. I needed time to collect my thoughts, to remember, if I was going to tell our story in peace, and without others insisting on adding their own anecdotes, like bricks and mortar, as if we were building a house together in which everyone could be comfortable.

∞

One morning in early March, Abel Tilliard awoke to the irritating whine of a chain saw. Immediately he felt a sickness growing in his stomach. He rolled out of bed, pulled on his pants and boots, and made his way out the back door, down the gravel path to the beach. As he buttoned his shirt, he thought he must be dreaming, but when he saw the towering maple topple toward the sea, he knew straightaway reality had become more sinister than his worst nightmare.

He watched two men wrap lengths of rusty cable around the stump, like a tourniquet twisted around a severed limb. A bulldozer struggled to pull the roots from the earth. The huge machine rose up in its tracks, but when the stump didn't budge, the few onlookers, men and children from the village, stood watching, bewildered and disappointed. They began to grumble. Tilliard felt a bitter jubilation. Then two men wearing hard hats moved the crowd back down the beach, behind a rope barrier. A whistle blew and the earth shook beneath their feet. Fragments of wood, rock and earth rained into the sky. The small group of locals who surrounded Tilliard cheered and clapped, and some thrust their fists above their heads. As the blast rippled across the bay and faded away amongst the islands and forest on the opposite shore, they pushed forward towards the crater. Tilliard watched one man heft his son onto his shoulders and say to the boy that what they'd just seen was like a comet exploding on impact with the earth.

Tilliard would have wept but for the anger, the disgust that cut into the edges of his memory. He wanted to do something, to say something about the senseless remark he'd just heard, to make it clear that another ice age was not an event you looked forward to with your children. He glanced into the eyes of his neighbours and wondered if they knew they had just attended an execution. The whole bloody lot were accomplices, were as dumb as posts, he thought. He despised them for their mindless celebration.

Refusing to turn around, to survey the desecration left by the explosion, he walked away slowly, back up the hill, fragments of images from the past whirling through his mind, blown skyward on the melancholy air. He entered his house and went to his bedroom overlooking the inland sea. He felt exhausted. A pain rose from deep in his chest and his tongue was sticky and dry against the roof of his mouth. He felt short of breath and took to his bed.

ॐ

When I asked him how long he planned to stay co-cooned in his room, he told me he could still hear the lower branches snapping as the tree smashed into the rocks of the beachhead. He heard the rings of flesh rip, the wound open. He smelled sap. And the trunk, he said, all six-and-a-half feet at the butt end, damn well exploded on impact.

Like a land mine, Rosie, he said. Like one of those land mines the Germans planted in the wheat fields overseas during the war. With one step, when your mind had wandered a million miles away, when your thoughts were at home with family or a girl you never expected to see again, with one careless step, your feet, arms, legs, torso would suddenly be flying off in all directions. He'd seen it happen, several times. Like parts of a puzzle, he said. Bits and pieces.

He winced. I wanted to rush to him, to cradle him in my arms and console him, but I knew that when he needed me most, he wanted nothing to do with me. His pale blue eyes clung to a dark time and space beyond the walls of this world.

And loud, he continued, loud enough to bust the eardrums out of a deaf-mute.

Night and day he heard the blast. Dynamite, he whispered under his breath, the bastards used dyna-mite. Later he swore he'd heard Eddie Drake's voice rumble through the thunderous explosion. He swore he'd heard someone call out his name.

His face screwed up as another spasm passed through his body.

What is it? I asked. Where's the pain?

In my bones, he said. It's as though the limbs of the tree were my own bones.

Hush now, I said.

Leaning over the bed, I placed my hand on his forehead.

You're not hot, I said.

I've not got a fever, he answered. It's my bones, Rosie, breaking. My ribs cracking. Again he grimaced.

He couldn't draw a breath without feeling pain.

∾

Would you read to me? he asked.

Wind gusts parted the curtains and bursts of morning sunlight angled across the room.

Now?

Yes.

What?

Rosie glanced at the magazine rack Abel kept beside the bed, then at the commode wedged into the far corner where she stacked her books. What would you like me to read? she asked.

It doesn't matter. One of your own stories. Anything. It's the sound of your voice I like. He closed his eyes. You used to read to me all the time.

Not for years now.

You stopped.

I thought you were bored. I thought my reading annoyed you.

You have a beautiful voice, he said.

Rosie picked up a book from the shelf, and without looking at the title, flipped to the opening chapter and began to read: "I am enfeebled by this torrent of light. Each afternoon seems the last for me." These were the opening sentences to one of her favourite books, but right away she regretted her choice. She should have been more careful, more selective. How could she have been so stupid? she wondered. She looked down and saw a smile creep onto his face. He was enjoying her discomfort.

Go on, he said. Don't stop! Just when you're getting started.

Rosie cleared her throat and continued.

As he listened, Tilliard saw her the night they first met, the night she and a friend, whose name he'd long since forgotten, walked into a summer dance at the village hall. This was before he and Eddie had signed up to go overseas. He noticed her long legs. Her calves were shapely but her ankles seemed too thick to let her move gracefully in the sandals she wore. He was wrong. While the band played, mostly Tommy Dorsey and Glen Miller tunes, they danced. And when the tempo of the music increased, she glided over the fir floor, lifting him out of his clumsiness. They moved well together, their legs and hips connected by the rhythms filling the hall. Months later, when they were married, Rosie told Abel that they'd been caught up in a circle of wordless desire. Music has that effect on people, she said.

The dress she wore that night was moss green with mother-of-pearl buttons running like a chain of small moons from her neck to her waist. Her lips were bright red, too red and full, he remembered thinking, against her tanned complexion, and her black hair fell freely about her face and shoulders.

They danced until his shirt was damp and her skin glistened.

I need some air, she said.

They made their way through the crowd, bodies caught up in the pulse of the music. At a table set up adjacent to the kitchen Abel grabbed two glasses of wine.

You're not from here, he said as they walked out into the night, the sound of the music, the trombones like ice melting, the solo trumpet like a golden whisper, teasing, the saxophones, bass and drums, now all muffled behind the closed doors.

We just moved into the McLean place, she answered. Next to the holly farm.

All the time they'd been dancing he hadn't thought to ask her name, so when he handed her a glass of wine and went to propose a toast, he hesitated, and then blurted out, To us!

My name's Elspeth, she said, an edge of wariness creeping into her voice. Call me Rosie. For my cheeks, my mother says. For the wind against my face.

Or for the wine we're about to drink, he said.

She laughed and wiped the back of her hand across

her forehead. He liked the way she made him feel at ease, as if what they said and did were willed, were part of a script they'd already written together. It was uncanny, he thought, watching her eyes, it was like looking into a set of mirrors and seeing recurring images of himself.

As he looked at her in the dim light cast by the streetlamp, he thought: This is it, everything we do, men and women, comes down to this. To what we want from each other, to what we value about ourselves, to the pride we place in our appearance, our bodies. The give and take. The expectations. The possibilities.

He took her hand in his and they walked down the hill, into the cooling breeze coming from the sea. The scent of arbutus blossoms, the devil's tree with its leaves falling all summer long, filled the night air. When they arrived at the maple, he told her this was his spot. Someday he would build a house above, overlooking the tree and the strait. All she could see was the trunk, a dark shape rising behind her, and the canopy of leaves that blocked out the star-filled sky.

He spread his jacket on the sand and the two of them sat, uncertain how to begin, where to begin, until she took his hand, placed it on her breast and kissed him, wet and searching.

What do you do? she asked. Your hands are so soft.

It's from rinsing glasses all day.

She looked at him, as if he'd spoken a riddle.

In the pub, he said. I work in the hotel for my father and uncle. One day I'll run the place myself.

Hearing a rustling sound above, followed by a noise

that sounded like someone washing windows, she turned away and glanced up.

Screech owls, he said. For as long as I can remember, they've been coming to this tree.

Do you think they're watching us? she asked.

Probably. Why not?

He paused and ran his fingers up and down the back of her neck, beneath her hair. They're supposed to be wise, he said, although he wasn't sure what he meant by this.

Maybe we would have more privacy in the boat, she said, nodding towards the white hull pulled up on the beach a short distance from where they sat. She stood, removed her shoes and stockings, unbuttoned her dress, pushed it down and stepped out onto the sand. Then she took off her slip. Fascinated by her boldness, Abel watched, unsure about himself, embarrassed. Then, so as not to be outdone, he stripped down to his shorts.

They launched the boat and Abel rowed out into the darkness, Rosie dragging her hand over the stern, rippling the cold water, to where they could no longer see shore and the only sound was the gentle lapping of waves against the hull.

Rosie held Abel, pulled him down on top of her.

I won't ask the obvious. She was breathing deeply.

What's that?

There was a silence before she spoke.

Are you happy?

I am, he whispered. And then he thought, that's not what she really wants to know. His heart beat faster. I do, he said, I do, and he felt her draw him in further,

her legs enclose him, and all of his uncertainty disappeared.

Afterwards they lay back, Abel feeling the imprint of the boat's ribs against his back, Rosie cradled in his arms.

Out here you feel as if you're floating in the sky, she said. The stars are the only way to tell which way is up.

I can show you another way, he said, and he thrust his hips in the air.

Don't ruin it, she said. Anyway, you should be so lucky. And then she pushed away from him. Besides, you need to save your strength for rowing, she teased.

Sit down, you'll tip the boat.

Which way's shore? she asked.

Listen, he said, you can hear the waves washing against the beach.

Then she turned, stood on the middle seat, and dove into the water, her feet kicking, leaving a phosphorescent trail.

Abel cursed, sighed and fell back against the bow of the boat. Further out he could hear the call of a loon. The current would carry him to shore. Already he could see the slightly darker shape of the tree against a lighter skyline.

The next day Eddie told Abel that he'd gone to the beach after the dance, to have a smoke and to drink one last beer before he made the trek up the hill and home to the farm. Funny, Eddie said, the fishing must have been good, the seals were slap happy, smacking the surface of the water. Lots of action. Such cries of joy I've never heard before, not coming off the sea. Must have been quite a feast. You know how sounds carry across water. Anyway, he said, their pleasure was my pleasure. Never had a beer that tasted quite so good.

A week later Rosie and Abel announced their engagement.

Rosie finished the paragraph she was reading, marked it with her finger and looked up to see Abel's eyelids fluttering, as if he were trying to keep pace with the individual images of a moving picture. She considered waking him, but instead closed the book and folded her hands in her lap. Men, she thought, take the weight of the world on their shoulders, even when they know it will squash them, even when the cause is hopeless. Like the story of the mouse trying to mount an elephant.

Tilliard dreamt of the tree. For more than fifty years, after a morning or evening of fishing, he and Eddie Drake had used the great maple as a landmark. When they were teenagers, Eddie would shovel cowshit out of the barn, hose down the stalls and gather eggs for his mother to sell at market. Only after he'd completed his chores was he allowed to meet Abel at the tree where they kept the boat and stored their gear. Eddie always had the smell of hay on him, and milk. He brought worms he'd dug, and he and Abel would bait their hooks before they headed out to the marker off the point. There they'd drop their lines and jig for cod. In later years, if they stayed out after dark, Rosie would hang out a storm lantern on a branch to guide them back to shore. They rowed their skiff lazily, relaxing into the anonymity of the blackness that surrounded them. They drank beer and talked about women or the most recent ball game down island. The maple stood solitary and invincible. Each ring of growth recorded another year the tree had weathered the sea's assault.

Propped up in bed, Tilliard viewed the beachhead, the tumultuous April sea, the islands and whitecapped mountains beyond, across the strait. All was blurred by the wetness in his eyes. He asked Rosie to pull the blinds. Grey, violent seas and the sight of snow chilled his bones.

When folks come to visit, he told Rosie, I want you to turn off the lights.

Who're you hiding from? she said.

No one's hiding.

She sat down on the edge of the bed and picked away at a loose thread on the eiderdown.

You prefer living like a mushroom?

No one should feel embarrassed on my account, he said. That's all.

Rosie shook her head. Hadn't he always claimed she had the bearing and disposition of a saint. Who better, then, than her to listen to what saddened him, but with age he had become grumpy and contrary when it suited him. He seemed pleased wearing a cloak of self-pity. She would have told him that he wasn't alone, but when she patted her thighs and told him to nestle his head into her lap he turned away and pretended to snore.

She was disappointed. You *have* become an old man she thought.

∾

I sat by the door and greeted neighbours who came to pay their respects. I told them that the tree's loss had left a hole in his heart, a hole into which his spirit sank. I said he despaired at the cavity carved in the sky by the tree's absence. Then I stiffened my back, pushed my glasses onto the bridge of my nose and pulled a thread through the needle-point pattern I was working. I was determined no one would notice how worried I was about the future. Nor did I want their pity, no matter how kindly it was given.

As friends took their places beside his bed—those who had known him longest nearest the headboard—they blinked their eyes and remarked they could barely distinguish his frail, ancient body shrouded in the darkness he now longed for. Everyone whispered, no one wanted to wake him from his slumber. Some brought gifts of home preserves and smoked salmon, and when they started to talk amongst themselves Tilliard sighed and said, I'm resting, just resting. What I need is peace and quiet. Besides, he said, it's not polite to speak behind a person's back, to pretend that a person's gone when he can still hear you speak. Remember, nothing is ever forgotten. Or forgiven, he said.

When his own children and his children's children entered his room, each carried a candle, and they heard him mutter that he felt as if he were watching his own funeral procession. Secretly they were convinced he had finally lost his senses, that he had deliberately set his mind into the concrete of perpetual delirium. Yet they were quick to reassure me that this was only a temporary illness. After all, hadn't Tilliard always had the constitution of a pack mule?

The family doctor, a young Scot, recently arrived and renowned for his herbal cures, came to the house. He diagnosed the problem as the flu and prescribed dandelion wine, plenty of rest, sunlight and fresh air. As the doctor packed his black bag, Tilliard whispered, so that everyone present could hear: I still think all sawbones are quacks, at half the cost. Of course I need fresh air and sunlight, he said, so did the bloody tree!

When he glanced up at me, his mouth curled into a smile, but I could see tears forming at the corners of his eyes.

Do you remember the story, Rosie, of the man who announced his own funeral? When his worst enemies turned up to pay their respects, he died laughing.

∾

The first sounds of spring circled the house, robins and hummingbirds, bees and flies. Rain tapped against the newly sprouted alder and dogwood leaves.

One morning, while Rosie was dusting the room—a task she'd always resented because, as she said, dirt waits for you—the doorbell rang. She returned to the bedroom, flustered, and spoke into the shadows.

It's him. He wants to have a word with you.

Who?

Tilliard's voice was distant, as if he were speaking from inside a rain barrel.

The young man from below.

Who?

The one who knocked down the maple, she said.

After a pause she heard movements beneath the bedsheets, like the sound of branches scratching on the rooftop. She heard Tilliard's breathing quicken. A curtain of blackness enveloped her. She wanted to run to the bed, seize Tilliard by the collar of his night shirt and rouse him from his lethargy; shake him so hard he could no longer indulge his bitter death wish.

Tell him I'm not in!

He knows you're here. The whole village knows you've taken to your bed.

Then tell him I'm not well enough to receive visitors.

Jesus H. Christ, Abel, not even he could have missed the parade that's trekked through your room over the last few weeks.

Tilliard moved his tongue deliberately along his cracked lips. A shiver began at the base of his spine, shot up his back and lodged in his scalp.

Get rid of the son-of-a-bitch! He paused, his voice weaker. Why is it, Rosie, why is it these days everyone's nose is stuck up someone else's arse.

Her eyes adjusted to the shadows and she saw her husband's frail head sink deeper into the pillow. His face had lost its tough, weathered tan. His cheeks were sallow, his eyes grey and heavy as a November storm. She went back to the young man, resentment welling up in her blood, a fist forming in her heart. She wanted to tell him he was an unwitting murderer, but as usual, whenever things went badly, she closed her eyes and took flight deep into the rain forest. Imagining count-less green shapes covered with moss, she shuffled through the dingy hall. As she neared the front door, she looked down at her wrinkled hands. Her fingers began to tremble, as if caught, like leaves, in a sudden October breeze. She felt a slight flutter in her breast as she confronted the young man at the door.

He's asleep, she said. Perhaps you could come back later. She hesitated, looking past him out to sea while he explained the reason for his visit, and then she closed the door without replying.

The small delicate flowers decorating her dress flowed about her body as she turned and retreated into the house. Some day she would tell the young man what she knew—she would explain her husband's decep-tion—she would let him know that Abel was a good man, a man who bought candy, three for a penny, for children in the village—a man who would give you the shirt off his back. But he could be stubborn, there was no question of that.

Her mind fell away to the timelessness of green.

∞

The years of fight were gone. At eighty-three, Tilliard knew what I feared to admit—that he would be the first to go. He was tired, he said, he was prepared for the end; it was his turn, he insisted, while I had my seven great-grandchildren to consider. Who else would tell them the stories they needed to know? Who be-sides me cared enough to tell the truth, as far as anyone knew it, about the terrible and lonely death of Eddie Drake?

Tilliard's concern for the fate of the great maple, older than the first families of the village, had become an obsession. He told me he had considered prayer for the first time since he was an altar boy; prayer had come back to him like a homing pigeon, he said, but the words seemed too simple to appeal to the biblical image of God he had formed in his mind over the past seventy-two years. Not since he was eleven, when he had said the Sunday service by rote with Reverend Cummings, had he believed prayer had the power to heal or change anything. Until recently he had thought the Almighty probably kept some sort of ledger in which He recorded the names of all those who had passed, long ago, beyond the path of spiritual salvation. Tilliard laughed. He took delight in imagining himself striding down the road to Hell.

Three, maybe four, months earlier, while we were sipping afternoon tea, he had told me our new neighbours were foolish to build so close to the sea. Salt would eat away the paint; mildew and fungus would spread their lingering decay into the soft wood. It'll be too damp, he said. During the winter when the weight of the sky closes down like a large grey lid, when the waters rush at them from above and below, they'll begin to believe they're living beneath the sea itself. And when winter storms roll around the island from the Pacific, tossing the misery of the sea onto their front porch, then they'll wish they'd built on higher ground.

You ought to warn them, I said.

Don't you think I want to?

He paused and fixed his gaze on my fingers as they drummed slowly on the oilcloth that covered the kitchen table. His face looked paler than usual, and his eyes peered at me, defiant and wounded, as if I were betraying him. He knew what I was thinking.

I would if I could, he said finally.

Then he stood, moved to the sink and rinsed his cup.

I watched him lean against the counter and stare out past his own reflection into the twilight, to where I knew the tree stood. I was certain he was shaping with his mind's eye what he was unable to see.

∾

When Rosie tiptoed back into his room, her round, metal-framed glasses set on top of her head as if she had an extra pair of eyes, Tilliard woke briefly and complained that his insides felt like a barren field. Rock and sand. Dead wood. His body gave off an acrid odour. He had wanted to strike out at the young man at the door, hit him, yet curiously he felt as if his spirit had received a reprieve, a special dispensation, which seemed odd to a man not the least bit religious. Do unto others, he muttered, do bloody well unto others. If he had his way, he'd take his revolver, his only souvenir from the war, point it at the bastard's head and pull the trigger. Then he felt his heart skip, flutter, and he gasped for air. All went black and he was positive in that moment of panic he was dying.

Tilliard's sleep was fretful. He imagined the young

man choked by the roots of the maple. His dreams wavered between a fear of an endless dark sleep and the memory of the day his new neighbours had begun to clear the land, the scrub brush, salal and small timber, in front of the house. He had watched anxiously to see if they would cut down the giant maple. They didn't.

One day, when he saw the young man surveying the clearing, Tilliard shaved, combed his thick white hair, and put on his Legion blazer. He carefully adjusted his beret, the one he'd bought in Paris at the close of the war, on his head. Grabbing his walking stick from the umbrella stand, he opened the door and marched out into the cold October sun. He walked down the path between the arbutus and wild roses. The young man stood like some divinity plotting his next act of creation. Tilliard resented the intrusion.

The two men stood side by side, watching the sea run ahead of the treacherous winds of a southeasterly. From this same spot thirteen years earlier, during the worst winter storm in memory, Tilliard had looked on helplessly as his friend Eddie Drake got caught in a turn of the winds, his small double-ender bursting into the air, Eddie's body sucked to the bottom like a bag of stones. If Tilliard had said it once he'd said it a thousand times, the silly bugger never should have been out on his own in the first place. The poor bastard couldn't swim; his steel-toed boots filled with water. And later, at low tide, Tilliard and others from the village had found Eddie anchored in a pool of seaweed and kelp, crabs crawling inside his clothes, his eyes staring, full of the sea.

This your place? Tilliard asked, his arthritic hands propped on his cane.

Pardon? said the young man.

You the one building the house?

Yes. He paused, then extended his hand. I'm Paul Coombs.

At first Tilliard ignored his hand, but then reached out only to be surprised by the strength of the grip.

Abel Tilliard. I own the hotel in the village. My family built the place in '27.

Why he volunteered this information, he wasn't sure. Perhaps it was important to establish a precedent, let the fool know his place. After all, wasn't it he who had slung beer to locals for sixty years? Who during the depression had organized a soup line at the kitchen door at the rear of the hotel? And who had given his name to one of the village roads? He took a deep breath of sea air before turning to gaze at the blue heron fishing a tidal pool.

I also own the place back of you here, he added, his left hand gesturing behind him.

Yes, I know, said Coombs. I've seen you at the window. Don't worry, I doubt the house will block your view. As you can see, we intend to build down below, close to the beach. My wife loves the sound of the sea.

It's a nice spot, Tilliard said. A good location.

He wasn't certain how to broach the subject of the tree. He glanced quickly at the youthful figure beside him; he searched the clean-shaven face for some sign of weakness, but all it revealed was a confidence that Tilliard thought bordered on impudence. He had always believed that a man's character could be read in his eyes, but now those eyes seemed to mock him, reflecting his own small figure. Coombs' clothes were too flamboyant, too casual. And Tilliard felt a bit foolish parading in his beret and Legion blazer. The gold brocade in the crest was, itself, too florid. But what did it matter, he was an old man, honoured in war. He leaned more heavily on his cane. He worried that when he spoke his voice would lack authority, confidence.

So, he said, his voice sounding high and faraway, the missus wants to build down below? Down by the beach?

Yes, Coombs said. She seems set on the idea.

Tilliard nodded. He stared down at his shiny black shoes, guilt flooding through his entire body. He wanted to tell Coombs to build back from the sea, but he couldn't bring himself to do so.

And what of the tree, he said. What are your plans for the tree?

Which tree? Coombs asked.

The maple. The large maple by the beachhead there!

None, I suppose. As you can see, we've left it standing. He paused, lifted his hand and shaded his eyes, as if looking at some distant object. It's a splendid specimen, now that you mention it.

Specimens are for bottles. Tilliard could feel the bitterness catch in his throat. That tree, he said, that tree's the one Eddie Drake and I used to tie the old double-ender to. Before he drowned.

Eddie Drake?

An old fishing buddy of mine.

I'm sorry.

We'd hitch a rope around that old maple because nothing, not even the goddamned sea, could pull its roots out of the earth. For fifty years we tied our skiff to that tree. And not once did she get away on us.

Coombs watched a flock of Bonaparte's gulls lift off the water and swarm towards the nearest island; then he examined his nails. When he looked up, Tilliard could see traces of a smile, and he was certain he sensed contempt behind Coomb's question. And you're asking me to leave the tree standing?

Tilliard tried to look calm. Yes, suppose I am, he said.

Consider it done, Coombs said, his hand sweeping the air with a magnanimity Tilliard distrusted. He felt cheated. It seemed resolved too easily. Nothing was free. He expected to have to give up something in exchange. His insides knotted, as if a burl had begun to grow on the wall of his stomach.

Tilliard had always fended for himself. He fished when he had an urge for salmon or cod. He dug clams and scoured for oysters weekly through the winter months. He was disgusted with the prospect of being indebted to anyone, especially a complete stranger, a man who owed him nothing. He never complained about the winter rains, the persistent dampness that invaded village existence. Even when the smell of mildew and damprot crawled onto his own body, lingered in his clothes and beneath his fingernails, he never protested. And in summer he praised the immensity of the clear blue sky that transcended all the measures of his knowing. Since childhood he had felt awed by the contemplation of distances and dimensions that took root in his imagination. Curiously, though, his reverence for distant galaxies had heightened his love of the mainland mountains, the islands, the bay, the beach and sandstone rocks worn and shaped into large toadstools by the tides, and most important, his love of the tree, the rambling old maple that shaded the beach. Without these landmarks, these touchstones, he would have been haunted by a sense of being anchorless.

A few days later Tilliard returned to the same spot to check on the progress of construction. The next thing he knew Coombs was standing beside him. The two men nodded at each other and then stood silently listening to the sounds of hammers and saws coming up from below. At last Coombs asked, Have you heard the story about the three men who were shipwrecked on an island?

Can't say as I have, Tilliard answered. This seemed neither the time nor the place to be telling stories. A cold wind blew from the northwest and he shifted from one foot to the other to keep warm. But I can see you have an itch to tell me, he said. Then he thought, if anyone tells stories here it should be me. He could tell Coombs about the rope swing he'd hung from one of the lower branches of the maple, how at high tide his kids had swung out over the water and dropped like kingfishers from the sky, he could tell him about the beach fires and drunken parties, or he could tell him what he'd never told anyone else, that one night after the war he'd crouched near this very place and heard Eddie confess to Rosie that he'd never marry, that he'd lost his ability to love, that he envied Abel, and he could tell him it was then he thought he saw Rosie hold Eddie in her arms and kiss him on the cheek several times. Tilliard had never said a word to her, as he'd say nothing now to Coombs. Stories were to be shared between friends and lovers. And sometimes, not even with them.

Go ahead, Tilliard said, tell your story.

Coombs smiled and rubbed his hands together. The collar of his leather coat was turned up but Tilliard noticed the lobes of his ears were still red.

One day a bottle washes up on shore, Coombs said, and when one of the three men uncorks it, a genie flows out, all smoke and eyes, weary, after being cooped up in the bottle for so many years. Centuries, let's say. Grateful to be free, the genie grants each of the three men one wish.

Sounds familiar.

You've heard it before.

No. Tilliard shrugged his shoulders. I have no memory for jokes.

Well, these three men are desperate. They've little water and food after being lost at sea many months earlier. They're living off the last of the rations from their life boat and what little they've been able to scrounge from the island.

Of course.

The first man, young and excitable, quickly explains that he has left a young girlfriend at home with whom he'd like to share a bottle of port, a warm fire, and a soft bed. Poof, he's gone.

The second man, older but no less appreciative, explains that he has a wife and family at home with whom he'd like to enjoy a meal and a pint of his favourite beer. Poof, he's gone.

The genie waits for the third man to make his wish, but he's surprisingly reticent. Finally the man says, I realize this may come as a surprise given our circumstances. I know it hasn't been all that long since they left, but I really do miss those two. I wish they were back here with me. Poof.

Coombs spread his hands and lifted his eyebrows as if to say, You see!

Some men are never happy, Tilliard said.

Exactly, Coombs said, without looking at Tilliard. My thoughts exactly. Coping with change is difficult.

As Tilliard awoke, these conversations with his new neighbour some six months earlier puzzled him. Why then had the son-of-a-bitch felled the tree? As the sleep cleared from his eyes he could just make out Rosie's face in the darkness of the room. His body ached and pain pierced his chest each time he drew a breath. Rosie leaned over him. He smelled garlic and wine on her breath. She set a candle on the night table and looked closely into his eyes.

So you're awake at last, she said.

I slept the sleep of the dead.

You were delirious. Tossing and turning like a man pursued by the devil himself.

Has he gone? Tilliard asked. Did you send him away?

Who? Rosie hesitated, amused by the thought. You don't mean the devil?

No, for chrissake, I don't mean the goddamned devil, he said. I mean that young bastard from below!

She clucked her tongue and then shook her head.

That was hours ago, she whispered, straightening the bedcovers.

Tilliard's dry, cracked lips began to tremble, and for the first time in weeks Rosie saw the old fury rise, clouding his face.

Why, he shouted, why in God's name did he have to take out *that* tree? No respect! The young have no respect. He did it deliberately. His arm rose and his hand struck out at the air, his finger waving at the ceiling. He couldn't wait until they carried me out of here in a fucking box? Was that so much to ask for, for Christ's sake? To Eddie's memory, I told him. What the hell could a couple of months, a couple of years at the outside, matter to him? May his heart burn in hell! And he promised, damnit. Promised!

His arm fell back to his side. Some people are short on honesty, he said.

Rosie bit down on her tongue. She knew every scar on Abel's body, but most of all she understood the scars on the inside. His remorse. His guilt. His pride.

His wife complained about the damp, she said quietly.

What?

For a moment Tilliard was silent. He clenched his teeth.

What? I don't understand! What the hell are you saying?

Shade. Too much shade. His wife finds the new house

too damp, and she thinks the morning sunlight might just take the chill off. She likes to sun bathe. Rosie tilted her head as if she were praying. He said to tell you that he'd tried to reason with her but she'd have none of his excuses.

Shade, he muttered.

Rosie nodded. She worships the sun.

Tilliard raised himself up onto his elbows. His tired joints cracked. Rosie heard him snort and she thought he was going to fly into a rage, but instead he threw himself back onto the pillow and laughed as she had never heard him laugh before.

Then, as suddenly as he'd started to laugh, he stopped and began rubbing his forehead.

The tree was a raft, Rosie, do you see that? A bridge maybe. Yes, that's it. A way of seeing the world. I'd forgotten that. All these years, this is what I've wanted to tell you. Between us. And he stopped at what he couldn't say; at what she knew.

Without warning, Tilliard flung back the covers, rose from the bed and walked to the window where he opened the curtains. Out past where the tree had stood was an evening sky full of stars. Never before had the stars seemed so bright. That he could name each and every constellation meant nothing to him, because for the first time he didn't fear the immensity of the space they filled. No longer did he fear what he could not see, what he could not measure with his eye. The moon shimmered on the cold spring sea, and he experienced a curious sensation of flight. He opened the window and heard the wash of waves on the shore below. The sound was simple and rhythmic, and he realized then he couldn't distinguish this music from the music that for the first time sang from the depths of his soul.

A bridge, he said.

ᐤ

I closed the curtains on the stars and the near-full moon and lay down on my bed in the pitch dark.

Tilliard never knew I had seen him follow me from the house that night, shortly after he and Eddie had returned from overseas. Nor did I tell him Eddie had asked me to meet him at the maple. What the war had done to that poor man is unrepeatable. Some experiences are better left wrapped in silence, even when they become what we fear most. Why terrorize others?

The weariness of a long day ached in my bones. I had left Tilliard standing at his window. I was relieved to see him breathing in the night air, not complaining of chest pains. At last he seemed reconciled to the tree's loss. I wanted to tell him that it was about time he learned to grieve, but instead I fell asleep. I drifted above a mountain stream, deep in the island forest.

The next morning I entered his bright sunlit room to find him lying in bed, his face shaved, hair combed, the beret perched on his head. His old body lay peaceful and still. I turned back the covers gently. He wore his Legion blazer over his pyjamas. I took his hands into mine. They were cold and pale like the moon. And then I leaned over him, lowered my cheek to his lips and listened.

As I reflect on what I remember, as I walk out of the forest tunnel, I realize there is a third type of man, a man who feels passionate about life; a man who feels the pain of people filled with promise; a man who'll go to hell to shelter those things that represent our longing to be rooted in the universe, forever. A man who'll go to any length to protect what he loves.

The Garden

As the woman approaches him in his garden, he recalls the line, "breathe deeply the gathering gloom." Darkness swirls around his feet. He is certain that if he pays this woman the slightest attention she will be annoyed. Yet a sense of vanity and erotic melancholy pushes him to the edge of humiliation.

Insane. He has never met this person before. Admittedly, she has a presence. Something which makes him feel effaced. A dread he can only explain as a lack of sunlight.

He wants to leaf-curl in on himself, find a disguise, as the conductor of an orchestra or as a foot soldier; as a blossom on a Yoshina cherry or as a frog in a pond. He longs to erase any resemblance he might have to the original words and blood of memory. He can feel a root in his mind tear, a sure signal that an invasion has occurred. There is a breach in his defences.

Her entrance is quick and thorough. He senses the

ground slipping under his feet. Trees speed by, fast forward.

She says she's a stockbroker. That she's in a hurry. She wishes to know everything he knows about gardens, about the virtues of mulch.

Her shoulder-length, auburn hair flies out from side to side, a counter balance to her bouncing stride. She tells him people in the village have described and praised his gardens. He is portrayed as an arboreal Monet, although no one has ever noticed him, brush in hand, standing dreamily before a canvas. Her lips part, seductively, he thinks, and a chuckle escapes between her white teeth.

He attempts to explain that he is just completing a meditation garden. He has not built it as a place in which to meditate but rather for what it might reveal to him about the nature of meditation. A spring breeze blows against his face. Why does he feel as if he is flirting with a scorpion whose tail will catch him in the confusion of his own hypnotic trance?

With a sweep of her hand she dismisses the clean, spare look of his new creation, plants isolated, alone, in their own patch of ground. Too much the sense of a still life, she concludes. She prefers the cluttered look, the fullness of an English country garden replete with vegetables and fruit trees, hedges and rose beds. Vegetation ordered but blended, balanced and manicured. A garden in full bloom.

He is perplexed. Has he not just told her that where they stand is at the centre of a new world? That the mulch will blend with the existing soil and the plants grow into each other over the seasons? Form released into infinite shapes through time.

She surveys his work, not with pleasure, but with politeness. As she turns, she points to an area beneath two towering Douglas firs. Appearances are the key here, she says. A garden is best when it can be left untended. Or, better still, abandoned. And it will still produce. Like a healthy stock. Blue-chip. Secure. With a high interest yield.

Inadvertently he is caught up in her enthusiasm and flair for enterprise. Briefly he feels aroused, a burning in his groin. Tears come to his eyes. He is shocked to realize that although they speak the same language, the words have different meanings. This realization increases his need to speak.

He bends forward and carefully prunes the candles on a Tanyosho pine.

Some things can't be rushed, he says, although he feels embarrassed by his spells of desire. He remembers what Francis Quarles said: "A fool's heart is in his tongue; but a wise man's tongue is in his heart."

He lifts a branch of full-grown Pieris to expose the delicate white horn of a Trillium. Take at least a year to know your garden, he continues, and then, even then, consider what you have beheld, what small fragment of the universe the shutter of your eye has glimpsed. For in the next moment, if night and dream have a place at all in our lives, you will feel the chill of recollection and know there was a time, a time when the order of the world called us beloved.

The woman turns and speaks back over her shoulder. You've lived too long in the shadow of your plants and trees. You're beginning to grow moldy. Where's the profit in that?

He smiles, for he knows he will be here long after she has departed. He imagines she will ride across the sky at the speed of light.

He wriggles his toes in the moss and feels the earth embrace his feet. There really is nowhere to go, he tells her, nowhere, but already she is climbing the hill, receding on the breath of wind that brought her.

Things Not Yet Said

Here's the crux of my problem. After the term break, early in the new year, I received a sealed letter, marked "Confidential," in my mailbox at the school where I teach. No one, not one of the secretaries, with the exception of Emily who doubles as receptionist, and not one of my colleagues would look me in the eye. Even Emily only glanced at me, ducked her head, wiped her eyes with a hanky and blew her nose. I had become the invisible man. In the Staff Room, when I went to get a cup of coffee, everyone in the room studied some object as if seeing it for the first time. Lamps, furniture, blinds, magazines, the clock, the notice board. They saw everything but me. Oh, I got a few gratuitous nods, but no exchange of the usual morning banter.

There are no secrets in the workplace. Admittedly, I'm as guilty as the next person when it comes to gossip. Rumors follow flight paths as reliably as migratory birds wing their way south for the winter.

When the bell rang to begin classes, I was the last to leave. I walked through the empty halls, past the rows of lockers, past the cabinet displaying all the athletic trophies the school had won, past the portraits of graduates and principals, to the band room. I had a spare in the first block and planned to do some grading, but I knew what the message in the envelope said, not word for word because I hadn't broken the seal yet, but I knew all the same.

Welcome to the new year, I thought. I climbed up on the podium at the front of the room, behind the lectern I'd salvaged from the demolition of St. Philip's, a defunct wooden church that had stood a mile or so along the old highway from where I live, and looked out at the empty chairs and music stands. At that moment I figured I could hear the Lessons read, the choir singing. I fingered the dark, polished wood and curved mouldings, made to look like a sculpture; it brought to memory the peace of church. Who in their right mind, I wondered, could dismiss music as an educational frill? As an alternative diversion for those too uncoordinated to play volleyball or badminton—sports the P.E. teacher, Renney, claims are for sissies.

In accordance with clause . . . of the Collective Agreement . . . we regret to inform you . . . and take this opportunity to thank you for your dedicated service . . . Sincerely . . .

I stuffed the letter back into its envelope.

Bankrupt. That's how I felt. I make no bones about it. My whole life seemed shredded. All the talk of cutbacks had trickled down to me. Music was expendable.

Jazz, in particular, was expendable. I was expendable.

Now, in mid August, two weeks before the new school year is to begin, I still haven't told my wife, Josie, that come September I have no place to go.

A week after receiving my pink slip, I walked into the band room and saw GIVE 'EM HELL MR SPENSER and WE'RE BEHIND YOU HUGH written in large chalk letters across the blackboard. I appreciated the students' support and in a moment of madness borrowed matches from one of them and burned my notice of dismissal in the wastebasket at the front of the room. When the flames were at their height I took my grade book and attendance register and tossed them into the fire. The students cheered. To say I was depressed and my behavior bordering on criminal would be an understatement. But I felt I needed to make some sort of gesture towards an authority that had lost all credibility with me. Fortunately, no one reported my actions.

After twenty-eight years of loyal service the bottom had fallen out of my world. I was being forced to take early retirement. That's what the Board decreed. Some ambitious minion had deduced I was eligible for pasturing if they stretched the age qualification by a few days. I assume this saved some senior administrator the unpleasant task of dreaming up a list of my shortcomings, in reality concocting reasons for substituting computer science for music.

As far as I could see, I was guilty of two things: I loved music, especially the way it entered through my pores and soothed my nerves, and I conveyed that feeling with some success to my students. They, too, wanted to play music, to disturb the silence; I wanted them to speak without worrying about being understood. Music made this possible. Through music they could chase their dreams without the hurt that was too often at the centre of their lives. My other flaw, I had been told by some of my colleagues and a few parents, was that I was too demanding; apparently my insistence on harmony, on the quaint requirement that everyone in the band play off the same page, was too dictatorial.

Wouldn't Josie have been surprised? Had she known of my reputation, she would have wanted to know who was smoking what. And had she known of my job situation, she would have demanded a public inquiry. She would have wanted to know who was responsible for letting go the best music teacher in the district. And she would have insisted I challenge my dismissal, thus pushing me onto a public stage that at that moment I desperately wanted to avoid. I'd grown weary of defending the arts against every incursion by the "relevancy" mafia. Besides, I never had unburdened myself with poise. So I told Josie nothing. With my early retirement package, my payroll deposits would continue through the summer into the next year—time enough to figure out how and what to tell her.

I hit rock bottom. Solid rock. I know, I know, what I'm saying is hackneyed, and perhaps if this is indicative of my state of mind, then I deserved to be let out to pasture. But would anyone feel better if I said I fell into an emotional black hole? Or that I was ready for an out-of-body experience? Just try standing, let alone walking, in my shoes, I said to Renney, who was the first to try to console me. See if that doesn't give you blisters or varicose veins. Everybody thinks it's so much easier to be somebody else, to live in someone else's skin, I said. Little do they know. If you haven't blown a few notes on someone else's horn, I told him, you ain't heard their tune.

What are the elements, I wonder, that give us shape, that contribute to the design that is us. Not necessarily how we see ourselves, not the genetic pattern either, but the whole being. The whole blessed human being. And does anyone give a shit?

Certainly not Ollie.

Ollie Pedersen, my neighbour on the west side, is not a friend. We abide each other. That's how he puts it. And that's pretty much how I see it. We've lived next door to each other for going on seventeen years and I know that when his herring skiffs are landlocked at the foot of his property and his trawler is docked for the winter at the marina down the bay, he writes poetry, rhymed poetry, and letters and articles for the local paper. As far as I can see, there isn't a topic he isn't willing to tackle. He prides himself on being knowledgeable on anything that pleases him. Or displeases him. I teach and write music, jazz mostly, and, over the years, his views on that subject have caused a certain strain in our relationship. He once claimed that jazz had nothing to do with music, especially what he heard coming out of the studio I share with Josie, who turns pots and sculpts—as if to mollify me, he said all jazz was noise, as far as he was concerned.

That pretty much sums it up.

We've talked to each other on maybe two dozen occasions, a few of those over the fence, a few over the phone, never over a cup of coffee or a few pints of beer. Once, and once only, he and I split the best part of a bottle of rum—and I've been suffering the consequences since.

We live in different worlds—Ollie and me—but a few weeks after I received my notice, when I was still dogged by self-doubt, while I was still feeling demoralized, as if I would never escape from the swamp of disinterested human kindness, we almost became partners in a project that I, unlike Josie, still think has some merit. Some potential.

One night, while we were washing the dishes, the phone rang. Josie answered. It's for you, she said.

Who is it? I mouthed.

How should I know, she said, too loudly for my comfort. Her facial features were calm, but telepathy told me she was pretending, that she was needling me.

I knew she knew.

When I heard the speaker at the other end, I didn't have a clue who it was. The voice was familiar, but I couldn't put a face to the voice.

Who is this? I asked.

Josie leaned against the kitchen doorjamb, her head bent forward, as though bracing herself against something predictable but unwanted; something not dangerous, but very likely stupid. Danger and stupidity often walk the same tightrope, she says, and often cause the same amount of pain.

The person at the other end of the line kept talking.

Finally I realized the voice was Ollie's, inviting me over to his place for a drink. Hearing his voice in the earpiece was as much of a shock to my system as it was learning via the grapevine that computer science had supplanted music on our local curriculum. RAM for Brahms, bytes for Bassie. I was prepared to lead the revolution. Luddites of the world unite. Anyway, Ollie said he had a proposal that would make us both rich. This offer came out of nowhere. As I say, we hadn't talked much, and certainly never about money. But I knew the last few fishing seasons had been tough for fishermen and, to my way of thinking, with what had happened to me recently, this made us allies. When I told Josie where I was going, that Ollie had some investment information he wished to share, she looked at me as if I'd just arrived from another planet.

Why, for God's sake, she said, when you've pointed out repeatedly that you have nothing in common with the man? No doubt she was irritated. What's wrong with you, anyway?

I don't know, I said. He may have something to say worth hearing. You know the old adage—when opportunity knocks. Besides, it's about time I behaved a bit more neighbourly. Got to know the man.

She wiped down the counter with a dishrag.

A wind out of the northwest, a good weather wind, rattled the windows.

She opened the oven and drew out the rack.

Do as you wish, she said. I sensed a note of contempt in her voice as I watched her busy herself pulling out pots and pans, measuring cups, an egg beater and a rolling pin from a lower cupboard.

Josie always bakes when she's frustrated.

The grass was damp underfoot, but all the same I stopped and looked at the full moon, pale and prophetic, rising out of the March sea. The air was filled with the smell of eelgrass and wet sand, the stirring of new life in tidal pools.

Ollie met me at the door, drink in hand. Mix your own poison, he said, as I stepped past him. There's rum and coke and a couple of swigs of gin on the table. Beer's in the fridge. He gestured to the end of the living room, to where the table stood at the junction with the kitchen. The cedar walls gave off a golden glow in the firelight. I poured myself a drink and tried to read the titles of a couple of the magazines scattered across the table. *Omni*, *The New Yorker*, and another that looked like it might be *Scientific American*. Not what I expected. Not at all.

Lifting his glass, Ollie proposed a toast to the miracles of modern science. I nodded at him and brought my glass to my lips. Science, I wanted to ask him, what do you know about science? But I was his guest and I felt obliged to hold my tongue. He motioned for me to sit down in a large wing-backed chair to the side of the fireplace.

You mean relativity, chaos theory, fractals, that sort of thing? I said.

He stood with his back to the fire and looked at me, quizzically. Of course, if he had asked me to expand on anything I'd just said, I would have opened my mouth, floundered, perhaps grunted, if not resorted to some form of intractable verbal antagonism. But he pushed his mop of red hair back from his forehead and emptied his glass.

Am I close? I asked. Time's arrow? I felt buoyed by his bewilderment.

I had no idea, he said, that you knew about this stuff. You're having me on! Right? He laughed. Time's arrow! Good one! He collapsed onto the sofa opposite me. Might use that image in one of my poems. I love the language of science. It embraces the world with such zeal, with all the freshness and enthusiasm of the evangelist. Don't you think?

I shifted in my chair and attempted to appear nonchalant. Hmmm, yes, I said, hadn't quite thought of it that way. But, yes, you might be right. I glanced across at him.

I knew it, he said. I had a feeling. In spite of our differences we think alike. He spread his arms along the top of the sofa.

What amazed me was that Ollie seemed genuinely impressed with my knowledge, with the terminology I'd cast out—more out of desperation than anything else. I'm not sure why, but I wanted him to think well of me—in spite of what Josie and I thought of him.

We watched each other, our eyes squinting against the dim light of the flames. And then, as if it suddenly dawned on him why I was there, he grinned and said,

But, hey, this isn't why you're here. He flicked on a lamp. You want to make some money, right? Big money! he said. Of course you do! We all do! He was already unrolling large sheets of drafting paper onto the coffee table that stood between us, each sheet containing a drawing that made as much sense to me upside down as it did right side up. A perpetual motion machine, he said, that's what's going to make us our fortune. I've already sunk twenty thousand into the scheme. Best investment I've ever made. Can't lose. Have a look at those drawings and I'll mix us another drink.

As he walked across the room, he said, Do you know anything about engines?

I studied the diagrams and shook my head. Not really, I said. Right away I knew I should've said, yes, that I had at least a working knowledge of the internal combustion engine. Ollie is one of those people for whom another's ignorance is a source of inspiration.

Figured as much, he said. Music's your thing. Jazz. Bebop. He gave a little twisting motion with his hips and chuckled. I love that sound, he said, love it, and he wagged his head.

I looked at the gold figure that stood on the mantlepiece. No doubt this was the statuette he'd picked up, just over a year ago, at the Golden Poet Awards in Reno. I couldn't remember the name of the Hollywood actor who was the patron of the event. For some reason, horror films came to mind.

That's all right, he said, I know enough for both of us. Besides it's the principle that counts here. Imagine an engine that doesn't pollute and is one hundred percent efficient. He handed me my drink and knelt down beside the table. Theoretically I could run my boat forever on the amount of fuel it would take to get her moving. There's a fortune to be made out of such a machine.

Ollie talked on about engines, his finger tracing over the lines on the paper. The inventor's a genius, he said, standing up and stretching his red suspenders with his thumbs. Professor Uli Petrov. He's from some place in eastern Europe. Lives in Edmonton now. Emigrated there after the war. Could have worked for NASA. He's brilliant. Absolutely brilliant.

Ollie paused and looked at me, his eyes wide open and laughing, challenging. He took my glass and filled it. While I felt uneasy, a pinch skeptical, I also thought, why not, the laws of the physical universe, as we understand them, are constantly challenged and changed. We're forever revising our creation myth. The perpetual motion machine might be the breakthrough of the millennium. We touched glasses.

But he needs support, Ollie said, as he paced in front of the stone fireplace. Our support. Yours and mine. He's low on cash. Governments and corporations don't fund what they don't want to understand. Or what might lose them a hold on a market they already control. They know the internal combustion engine and that's that. They're on fossil fuel overload, backing an engine that at its best is only thirty-five percent efficient.

His voice was lower, almost a whisper. He bent towards me.

Friction, Ollie said, Uli's found a way for us to live

almost friction free, outside of a vacuum. We don't need to be in outer space. His application will work right here. Ollie pointed at his carpet. In those sketches and drawings, he said, is the evolution and perfection of the perpetual motion machine. He showed me a cardboard mock-up he'd made from Professor Petrov's drawings and told me he'd almost duplicated Professor Petrov's experiments, right there in his own living room. He said Professor Petrov hoped to have a working model of the machine ready within a couple of months, but he needed capital.

Ollie stared at me, looked directly into my pupils. That's where we come in, he said. We can help finance one of the great discoveries of human history. The elimination of friction in the mechanical universe.

The room was warm and I felt my face flush. My instincts told me everything Ollie said was unbelievable. My brain was swimming between slot machines and the perpetual motion machine. Between some remote concept of a Protestant God haboured in the recesses of my brain and the cosmos according to this distant relative of the Norse pantheon. But I'd be the first to admit my skepticism had been washed away by the booze and even more so by Ollie's enthusiasm. I noticed the bottle of rum was almost empty.

So you're confident this engine will work? I said. My words sounded formal, my voice tight in my throat. Distant.

Absolutely, he said, no doubts at all. Can't miss.

We sat in the glow of the fire and drank off what remained in the bottle, the two of us congratulating each other on being pioneers in science and technology. For being open-minded entrepreneurs. We compared ourselves to Galileo and Copernicus, Ford and Daimler. Only we were bigger. The mission we were about to embark on was huge. Cosmic. According to Ollie it was only a matter of time before we'd be travelling at the speed of light. To other galaxies, he said. No question, he said. No question at all.

While I wrote out a cheque, for a sum far greater than we could afford, I envisioned Josie and myself, risen from the pedagogical ashes, riding around, hair windswept, in a new Mercedes roadster.

You won't regret this Hugh, he said.

I nodded, shook my head, then stood up, grabbing on to one wing of the chair. I felt an exhilaration I hadn't experienced in years and slightly sick to my stomach.

I was drunk. I have to go, I said.

We shook hands. My palms were damp and I could feel my face flush.

Partners, he said.

Yes, I said, but I didn't tell him Josie would resist the idea. Nor did I tell him that at the moment I was a bit low on cash. That my future was not exactly a cozy prospect.

As I stumbled back to the house, I looked up at the full moon. It had shrunk since I'd seen it earlier. It was cut up by the firs that grew along the beach. The stars had shifted and I had some difficulty picking out my favourite constellations, but I felt good being such an intimate part of the universe.

The following morning, over coffee, Josie confronted me. Why had I come sneaking back into the house so late. Smelling like a booze-hound to boot. I told her all about the perpetual motion machine, about Professor Uli Petrov, about the twenty thousand dollars Ollie had already invested in the scheme. I told her I thought we would be wise to get in on the ground floor. And I told her about the cheque I'd written.

When I mentioned the cheque I was certain I detected her gasp and stagger backwards. Then she walked to the phone and dialed a number.

Hello, she said, I'd like to speak to someone about putting a stop order on a cheque my husband wrote last evening. She explained that there had been a misunderstanding, that we didn't have sufficient funds in our account to honour the cheque without her authorization. And, she said, more emphatically than I thought was necessary, that wouldn't be forthcoming.

Who's the cheque made out to? she asked.

I jerked my thumb towards Ollie's place.

Josie rolled her eyes. A Mr. Ollie Pedersen, she said.

When she got off the phone, she sighed and tapped her forehead. Have you taken leave of your senses? What you did is crazy. You're crazy. You know that? Certifiable, she said. And it's not just the money that's at issue here. The science is impossible. High school physics ought to tell you that! But, pardon me—and here she hunched her shoulders and spread her arms out— you flunked high school physics, didn't you? And every other science course, as I recall. That's what attracted me to you in the first place. While everyone else wanted to be an engineer, you were happy playing the saxophone. You wanted to be an artist. That's why I found you sexy.

That was thirty-five years ago, I said. Since then I've watched my share of TV. Plus I've done some reading. (I knew I was grasping.) I looked out the kitchen window at the plum trees coming into bud. What's sex got to do with it?

But did you understand what you watched or read? she asked. She waited for me to say something. Apparently not.

She stood up and walked down the hall to the bedroom. I followed her.

That's the problem, I said, on her heels like a bloodhound, always has been. All great discoveries challenge existing laws. Remember Galileo? Copernicus? You have an original idea and the rest of the world wants to see you burned at the stake.

But they were scientists, Hugh, not musicians. They knew which end of a telescope to look through.

She lay down and folded her arms over her forehead. I wanted to remind her that it was me, not her, who had the hangover. Her eyes were covered.

I'm sorry, Hugh, but sometimes you can be so—I don't know—so utterly hopeless. My God.

Over the next week, Ollie phoned me at least once every night. How was I doing? What had happened to my cheque? He'd received a stop-payment order when he went to deposit my cheque in his bank. While he understood that consultation was sometimes a necessary part of marriage, towards the end of the week he started to get more personal: When was I going to liberate myself from Josie's apron strings? Become my own man?

I stalled him as best I could. I pleaded with Josie. I suggested to her that we might be passing up on the chance of a lifetime. Our only opportunity for early retirement.

Stick to your music, she said. Don't be such a damn fool. Her voice became soft and gentle, caressing. You know who you are, that's all that matters. She paused as if I'd missed her point. You're a fine musician and your students love you for it. I love you for it.

I told her she was being unreasonable. Stubborn. That it wasn't the idea at issue here, it was her dislike of Ollie.

Right away she resented what I'd said. She ignored me. After a few days of the silent treatment, I came in from my studio in the evening and heard her on the phone. She was saying we wouldn't be investing in any such foolishness. And, no, I wasn't a spineless something or other and that he'd best stop calling. Her voice was firm. I heard her say that, no, a handshake was not as good as a written contract, especially when made between two men who had more drink in them than they could handle.

I stood by the door. Listening. Josie turned and saw me. Her face had that expression on it which said, don't worry I've got everything under control. I have to admit that I was relieved, although I also felt a loss. But I wasn't sure what it was I'd lost. When she hung up, Josie watched me. I didn't know what to say. I was amazed by her calmness. No anger, nothing. She walked over and kissed me on the cheek.

It's over Hugh, she said, and then went to sit in her large, stuffed chair and work on her crossword puzzle. I went into the living room, flicked on the TV and watched the weather report and sports roundup.

I love Josie—we've been married for over thirty years— and as I sit here on the lawn in the fullness of the noon-day sun, I think about the nature of trust, about speaking one's mind versus the need, at times, for diplomacy. In jazz you simply improvise, let your voice speak, usually in unison or harmony. When there is equivocation, discord, it's resolved. Otherwise you are left with cacophony, noise—with nothing more than unpleasant noise.

A couple months later, at lunch time, during one of our weekend planting binges, Ollie stomped onto our front porch, marched up to the screen door, and peered in at Josie and me sitting at the kitchen table. Follow me, he said. Not so much as a hello, how are you. With one swoop of his arm he hooked the two of us and we dutifully followed him back to his place, through his carport, to his side of the fence we share.

His voice boomed. What do you think that is? he asked, pointing his finger with all the authority of a Nordic god.

Josie and I stared at the junk he had piled up against the fence—pulleys and poles, an old chain and anchor for his boat, piping, a ladder, rusty fishing equipment, odd lengths of rope and lumber—and we stood there, like two disobedient children, waiting to hear what it was we were supposed to have done. Wondering what it was we were supposed to be looking at.

Dirt and weeds, he said. You've been throwing your goddamn compost on to my side of the fence. Covering my stuff with your rubbish. What do you think this place is, a dump?

For a moment I was worried Josie might answer that question. She can be blunt. I thought she might say something about the fish ponds he'd filled in, about the azaleas and rhododendrons he'd bulldozed under when he decided to turn the rock gardens and paths the previous owners had lovingly created into a tiny pasture for his most recent wife's horse. (He's been married three times that I know of and only a few months back we heard the latest one had packed her bags.) From the start I'd known it wasn't going to work. A horse needs more room to run.

Josie believes Ollie suffers from an overdeveloped libido and she's never forgiven him for what she calls his diabolical nature. Late one afternoon, a few years ago, while listening to a radio drama, she watched him throwing bread crumbs to the Canada geese that swim along the sea shore in front of our houses. After he'd gained their trust and had them eating out of his hand, he grabbed two, one in each hand, and snapped their necks. Josie was furious. She said she could hear their necks breaking from the sitting room. When I tried to tell Ollie how upset Josie was, he offered to bag me a bird for Thanksgiving dinner.

Ollie's a hunter, I'm not. He has guns, I don't. On occasion, for no apparent reason, except I think he knows weapons of any sort unnerve me, he fires them at the sky. He learned of my fear one day, shortly after we moved in, when he shot an arrow just over the roof of my car as I came down the driveway we share with two other families—he'd set up a bull's-eye target, at least six feet below road grade, against a bale of hay. As an arrow whizzed past, I yelled at him, told him he was an irresponsible prick. He apologized by telling me he'd accidentally missed his target. Accidentally? I said. By twelve feet? Then he wondered if I'd like to have a go. I declined. He waved his hand, raised one eyebrow and said, Suit yourself. A man's got to do what a man's got to do. This remark annoyed me, partly because he's younger than I am and partly because I'm convinced he thinks my virility, my manhood, is an issue.

I watched Ollie as he stared at the fence and then at the piles of junk he'd tossed aside. His own precious archaeological quarry, out of sight, out of mind—until now! He kicked the ground and then rubbed his chin. I wanted to ask him what Josie and I were doing there, but before I could say anything he made a wild gesture with his arms. Like a tilt-a-whirl run amok.

So, he said, why you throwing your refuse onto my property? I thought you guys were into organic gardening. Don't you have a compost bin?

We have, Josie said, folding her arms across her chest. He didn't hear.

163

This is bullshit, he said, speaking right over her words, bloody bullshit. Organic gardeners, my ass! He gave a twist and a tug up on his jeans.

Josie and I were dumbfounded. We both stood there, glued to the spot, being bullied.

But we have no garden on our side of this section of fence, I said.

So you cart your rubbish over here from somewhere else, probably from your vegetable garden, he said, and fork it onto my side of the fence because you know I'm away fishing for most of the summer and I'm not likely to look here before everything rots. That's devious, he said, fucking devious.

I bent over and ran the soil through my fingers. This is potting soil, I said, we don't use potting soil.

He stared at the small sample I held in my hand and said, What are you trying to tell me? Go on, say it. That you had nothing to do with this? Go ahead, don't be bashful. Doesn't suit you. His watery blue eyes narrowed to slits, his cheeks reddened. He was keyed up, tight. His breath came in quick gusts in the afternoon sunlight. Never did trust teachers, he said, especially music teachers. When I turned and looked at Josie I saw that she was almost apoplectic. Her lips moved but no sound came out. I followed her gaze to the back of his house. Lined up along the wall were at least twenty to twenty-five garden pots, all drying in the full southern sun. I was choked.

See those? I said. I pointed with my fist. Those! I jabbed the air. Over there, by the house!

He moved his head slowly from side to side, as if by changing positions he might get a better understanding of what it was I was asking. Who do they belong to?

His eyes followed the line of my arm. He shrugged, grunted thoughtfully, and said, My tenant I guess.

He turned and looked at me, as he revealed this self-evident truth. Who else would it be? he asked, scratching his head.

Josie grabbed me by the elbow and guided me towards the front yard. I don't know what she thought I might do, why she felt she needed to usher me away. Perhaps she thought I would do or say something I might regret.

What a prehistoric ape, she said, as we climbed over the fence, back to our place. He's such a bitter, scheming little weasel. And he takes so much pride in his ignorance. Dead in the head, that's what we used to say about people like him. Dead wood.

The next time I saw Ollie was across the fence. I waved, but he thrust his arm and finger towards the sky and shouted something I couldn't make out for the wind blowing his words back in his face. All I could hear was the squabbling of gulls and crows.

The truth of the matter is, with fewer and fewer opportunities available in which to offer Josie an explanation, I have to wonder why I spend so much time thinking about what might have been. About what to do with the rest of my life. These days I'm always scheming, hoping for a vision that will alter history, destiny, that will land me a gig as the lead horn in a successful band. Or will place me back where I most want to be, in front of a group of high school students who are as excited about jazz as I am. My God, I want a miracle.

Josie accuses me of smothering my passions, of not taking control of my life. Which, she says, occasionally includes hitting out at the world. Ass kicking, she says. I'm too docile, too timid. I could argue that a hot sun saps my energy, leaves me fatigued, but Josie'd ask what accounts for my behaviour the other nine months of the year. Out on the tidal flats a dog chases gulls, back and forth, back and forth. Splashing and barking. I'm in love with the futility of its pursuit. There's pure joy, I point out, but Josie has her back to me, and is bent over pulling weeds and listening to her Walkman.

She seems more easily aroused these days, after her passage through menopause. She says her heightened interest in sex is the result of her increased testosterone level. One of nature's little ironies. Arouse the female at the same moment the male would be happiest in a hermitage.

I'm confused. Josie's affection terrifies me. I'm in love with a woman with whom I can't speak. With whom I want to share what in my heart I know I wrongly consider my shame.

As I say, we live in different worlds. Ollie in his, we in ours. This may sound like an exaggeration, but it's not.

The night after our encounter over the compost, just after we'd turned out the bedside light, I whispered to

Josie that I heard a scratching sound by the front door. Leave it be, she said. Go to sleep. It's late, she said, and rolled over. Within minutes she was snoring lightly. I couldn't put the matter out of my mind. At first I thought it might be Tobias, Ollie's tabby cat, looking for a bowl of milk—Josie often gives Ollie's cat an after-dinner snack and a petting—but it was too late for him to be visiting. Then I thought it might be the sea otters returning, searching for a way back under the front porch. Last winter they'd set up home there and the stench of rotting fish had almost driven us out. I tried dancing on top of the deck, shining lights underneath from all sorts of different angles, and playing music. Loud music—classical, jazz, rock. Nothing made them budge until I ripped up several boards. Then they shot out from under the porch as if fired from a canon. They slid across the frosty planks leading to the beach and scooted the final few feet to the water. A hundred yards or so from shore they surfaced and looked back at me, waiting for me to disappear. Taunting me. I hid around the corner of the house for a few minutes, then sprinted out front. Sure enough, the whole family was working its way towards shore. I waved my arms, fanning the air. Again they dove under, a trail of bubbles showing their path away from the beach. Again they came up looking back in my direction. Terrorists. I knew they would return, so I sprinkled lime over the whole area to kill the smell of shit and rotting fish, and nailed up a lattice skirt to keep the little buggers from getting back under.

But on the night of the potting soil incident I was

too tired to get up and drive otters or anything else away. Next morning, while I was shaving, I heard Tobias meowing outside. When I opened the screen door I found six cans of tuna stacked on the steps. There was no note. Nothing. Just six cans of tuna.

Josie wasn't surprised. What did you expect? she asked. It's human nature, she said. Nobody likes to admit they're wrong. That they've made a fool of themselves.

A few scribbled words, I said, I would have appreciated a few words.

I placed the cans in the kitchen cupboard.

But, I said to her, this will have to do. It's better than nothing. Right?

Josie listened, then shook her head, slowly. Would it make any difference? she asked. Would an apology make any difference?

To whom? I wanted to ask her. As far as I was concerned, it would—and it wouldn't—depending on your point of view.

Yes, I said.

She took one of the pots she'd brought in from the studio the previous evening and held it up to the sunlight streaming in through the kitchen window.

Perhaps not for you, I said, but for me, I think so. Yes it would. His admitting that we were right, that he wronged us, might make a difference.

Oh, she said, eyeing me with a hint of disappointment.

I watched her examining her ceramic bowl.

Sometimes, she said, turning the bowl to look at it

from different sides, things not said are less important than what a person already knows. She paused. Her lips curled up at the corners of her mouth. Then again, often things not yet said are best left unsaid. Don't you think?

As usual, whenever she was annoyed with me, Josie spoke in riddles. Koans. Who could blame her? I wanted to tell her I wasn't the milquetoast she thought I was. But therein lies a whole world of potential misunderstanding.

Then she opened her hands and dropped the bowl on the hardwood floor.

I winced.

It was cracked, she said. Spoiled, she added, in spite of appearances. I didn't mean to startle you.

But you did, I said, shuffling from one foot to the other. I was sore that she felt the need to get my attention this way.

Wiping her hands on her apron, she stepped over the pieces of pot scattered across the floor, circled her arms around my neck, and rested her head against my cheek.

When you play your horn, you sound like a man for whom music is his pulse, his breath. You sound like a songbird. With people you are hopeless.

I don't understand, I said.

You're not exactly the best judge of character, she said.

Then she held my chin and kissed me, softly, wetly, full on my mouth. Her hold was strong.

I felt aroused by the warmth of her body against

mine. When she opened her eyes, her sea-blue eyes, I wanted to say to her that no matter how insolent, stubborn, or stupid a person is, no matter how gullible, no one deserves to be alone, no one. No matter what. Instead I found myself looking into a well so deep I felt dizzy. I felt as though I were looking into the eyes of a complete stranger.

How to tell Josie that at moments like this I feel abandoned?

This is not at all how I want things to be.

Hold me, I want to say, hold me. I am not ready to be old.

As I watch Josie stroll across a sandbar, climb over logs and up from the beach, a few sand dollars clutched in her hand to add to her collection, she is the picture of composure, of control. For her, all is right with the world, everything in synch, everyone in their place. On a hot August afternoon, I should not feel unhappy about her unrestrained optimism—she is, in her fifty-first year, a gem—but nagging at the back of my mind the fact remains, in two weeks' time I have no place to go.

What Men Know About Women

Nothing. We know absolutely nothing, my friend Gus said in response to one of my son Eric's searching questions, questions that came like missiles out of nowhere and seemed impossible to detect, deflect or answer. We were on the I-80, driving between Cheyenne and Salt Lake City, then on to Portland and north, up the coast, home. When it comes to matters of the opposite sex, Gus said, we're creatures with two minds pulled in opposite directions.

He said this when we stopped for breakfast, at one of those truck-stop diners where you get a couple of eggs, sausages, bacon, hash browns, and a stack of pancakes drowned in maple syrup. And enough coffee to idle away a good part of the morning in conversation.

This is the memory I have as I lay Richard Ford's *Rock Springs* on the bedside table and switch off the reading lamp. My wife, Jean, is asleep. Gus would say she is a

case in point, our relationship typical, a perfect illus-
tration of what he's saying. I'm lying on top of the covers in the dark, she's between the sheets. Gus would
say this picture of domestic bliss is pretty much self-
explanatory.

I listen to her breathing, which is heavy and slow.

The fact is, we never seem able to get our lives into
synch. One or the other of us is asleep while the other
is awake. Every weekday morning, Jean rises early,
downs a cup of black coffee and a couple of pieces of
toast, and drives to the animal shelter where she does
volunteer work for an hour or two before she goes on
to her own office. She's a veterinarian. After she leaves
the house, I lounge in bed and try to make up for sleep
I missed the night before. I lie back and dream about
other lives, about things that could have been done
differently. Jean is right. I have a tendency to put a
reverse spin on events, to see life as darker than it is. I
don't know why that is. Habit perhaps. I can find the
unholy on a perfectly sunny day, when the sky is clear
and blue from horizon to horizon.

As I say, I've just this minute finished reading Richard Ford's collection of stories. I like what I've read, the
effortless voice, much of the action and many of the
insights, but I have some difficulty warming up to some
of the people, especially someone like Earl Middleton
in the title story. I feel uneasy about his ambivalence,
his difficulty with what's right and wrong, his problems with women—he's totally at odds with himself
when it comes to Edna—and the ease with which he is
willing to hot-wire a cranberry-coloured Mercedes and

beetle off towards the I-80 and on down to Florida. He has too many excuses for my liking. He treats his daughter Cheryl well, which as a father and family man I appreciate. I guess Earl has certain virtues that some readers will like, but to my mind he's too much like other members of my generation, the sixties crowd, who are far too quick and willing to give in or up.

Now, just when I imagine I'm all alone to dream as I want, I feel Jean turn away from me, hear the rustle of sheets as she settles back in, on her stomach. After all the years we've been together I can't imagine how anyone can bear to sleep that way. Face into the pillow. I'd smother. Jean says it's my insecurity, that I'm always watchful, which is why I have to lie on my back. Alert.

I concentrate on my heartbeat, wait until everything is still. Quiet. So I can refocus.

What strikes me most about Ford's story is the way he captures the place, and with so few details. As I read the stories I feel like I'm right back there in Rock Springs, with Gus, another friend's son, Jamie, aged twenty-one, from England, and my own son, Eric, who was nine at the time. This was back in 1989.

We drove over the Rockies and across the prairies to Winnipeg—with a stop in the Badlands at the dinosaur museum in Drumheller, a dry dusty bowl of a place, nestled down out of the wind, so Eric could visit what he called either the deadlands or bonelands, I forget which. Like most kids his age, Eric was in love with large lizards, even when he was forced to imagine their shape from a skeleton, while for me history seldom stretched back past the last monthly sales reports (I'm in real estate and insurance) or my wife's most recent and willing fulfillment of our marriage vows. I tend to respond to whichever came last or more frequently. Eric got his fill of large bones while I walked about the place feeling not only inadequate but envious.

As I gazed out over a recreation of a scene depicting Triceratops and Tyrannosaurus about to do battle, I wondered once again whether or not I was guilty of concealing my true feelings. There were times—while driving to work or walking through the mall or eating a soufflé or listening to John Coltrane or watching Jean slip into her lingerie—when I fantasized about making love. On the sofa, in the shower, in a Jacuzzi—in all the obvious domestic locations—and in a gondola on a Venetian canal during a rainstorm. I imagined teasing the fine hairs on her arms and the inside of her thighs. Goose bumps rising, from the cold and anticipation.

Thoughts of sex like daydreams have a way of drifting to the mind's surface in the oddest places. For the past six months I'd been aware of a sense of urgency I needed to escape. While I'm not one to keep a daily record, it seemed to me sex had become an all-too-infrequent occurrence in our lives. One of my fears was that I would no longer be able to arouse Jean. She said I was overreacting, that like most men I had no appreciation, no understanding, of what women wanted. No idea of the mysterious metamorphoses women went through. She got no argument from me on that score. I didn't know.

After Winnipeg we swung down through Fargo and on to Minneapolis where my daughter, Shelley, was playing in a soccer tournament.

But for all four of us boys, the trip began after we'd covered the first sixteen hundred miles, as we prepared to cross the border into the States, into a foreign country.

At the end of the rainbow, beyond the shadow of doubt, beckoned Paradise. Or so we thought. But the invisible line, the longest unprotected border in the world, became a rapidly shrinking portal. A gateway booby-trapped with regulations. Jamie, who had flown over from Manchester only two weeks earlier, ran into some problems with his British passport. He didn't have a visa, and an over-zealous customs official, a model of individuality and personal discretion, was ready to ship him back to England. Needless to say I was annoyed. I'd promised Jamie's dad, a business associate, I'd show his son a chunk of the good ol' US of A. Suddenly he was at risk of having his trip terminated, all because of some bureaucratic sleight of hand. For three-and-a-half hours we were stuck in a no man's land between two countries while Gus and I tried to make the point that we were not dealing here with a citizen from a hostile power.

No matter, the customs woman said. Young or old, friend or foe, everyone needs a passport, or a passport and visa, to enter the United States.

I've noticed that sometimes the uniform defines the man. Well, in this case the uniform defined the woman.

I'd be lying if I didn't admit that she was attractive. She had raven-black hair, drawn tight against the sides of her head and bundled up in a bun in the back, which gave her an appearance I sensed was a deliberate denial of suggestion. And green eyes, beautiful jade eyes, that reminded me of Jean's. And like Jean she wasn't going to be put off her pace, her routine. She smiled, self-satisfied, and I gazed around the pale, rose-tinted room she used as a holding cell for those lost souls she considered possible vagrants. There were a few photographs on the walls of men I didn't recognize, local or state politicians I figured, a wooden bench, a couple of metal-framed chairs and a counter that divided the room.

The smell of diesel exhaust mixed with the scent of dry summer grass wafted through an open window.

When she asked which one was my son, I stood behind Eric and put my hands on his shoulders.

She smiled again. On summer vacation, are you? She looked at Eric.

Eric nodded and shuffled away from me, as if he'd just been touched by poison ivy. He shifted from one foot to the other, alternately rubbing the toe of one Nike with the sole of the other. I could tell he was annoyed that I'd made him wear shorts.

That's cool, she said, giving him the thumbs-up. Lucky you. She pointed to his shirt. I like the Bulls, too.

Eric glanced up at me contemptuously. We'd also argued that morning about which shirt he should wear, for no good reason that I could think of, but which had seemed critical to both of us at the time.

I felt my face flush. First I was deserted by my own

178

son, then a complete stranger had managed to widen the wedge between us and gain his confidence. Eric walked over to the door and stood, back hunched to the room, hands in his pockets, in a shaft of sunlight. I could do nothing but wait. Parenting, I had told Jean in a fit of blazing illumination and self doubt, is the art of not missing missed opportunities. And there are few of those, I added.

Jamie, who appeared amused by the proceedings, produced a smile that Gus and I were to learn later he could switch on in any situation that smacked remotely of crisis. And his speech tended to tranquilize people. His short phrases coupled with his Lancashire accent made him sound like some sort of exotic songbird. But this time when he spoke his charm fell flat. The customs woman's forehead furrowed and she looked at him without comprehension. I wanted to tell her her attitude needed work, but I didn't want to have to turn around and go back the way I'd just come either.

No matter what we said, she either didn't hear us or wasn't interested in hearing us. Gus leaned on the counter, perhaps invaded her space a little, who knows these days, and attempted to cajole her. He told her a joke I didn't hear. When she laughed out loud I got my hopes up, but then she continued right on typing our passport numbers into her computer. Gus turned and shrugged his shoulders. We're not in a hurry anyway, he said, looking at me for confirmation. This is supposed to be a holiday, right? He walked over to one of the large plate-glass windows and stared out into the parking lot.

We could be those poor bastards over there, he said. I joined him at the window. Jamie lingered at the counter and pretended to read through a brochure on immigration while eyeing our hostess from behind a long lick of streaked brown hair.

Across the way two men in uniform had pretty much disassembled an older Ford van. Suitcases, sleeping bags, a mattress, a pile of clothing, a cooler, seats, spare tire, a jack and door panels were piled up around the vehicle. A pale, thin woman, sunglasses pushed down on her nose, stood with her hands on hips and appeared ready to box someone's ears in. That's one unhappy camper, Gus said. Her travelling companion squatted on a nearby curb and smoked a cigarette. I couldn't make out if it was a man or woman, not that it mattered.

That could be us, Gus said, you realize that?

Not quite, I answered and walked back to where I'd been sitting. Different mix of people. Older vehicle. Appearances, I said. That's what seems to matter as much as anything else here.

The woman behind the counter sighed, glanced up at me and shook her head, then looked at Gus and smiled.

Gus is a big, blond-headed man, a diesel mechanic by trade, with a good sense of humour. He's got all those qualities people seem instantly drawn to. Freckles, dimpled smile, good teeth, a nose that was broken when he was a kid and was never straightened, and a laugh that rises right up out of his boots. Not much penetrates his defences. By contrast, I have little patience for stupidity, especially when it's coupled with stubbornness. I figured we were up against both.

In spite of Jamie's and Gus's attempts at diplomacy, this woman seemed, at least to my mind, determined to hold us to ransom. We could rot away in this little private hell of hers between countries. She was in control, not so much of us, but of the space. Of some idea this space represented. Something greater than a few yards of dirt.

The smell of disinfectant hung in the muggy air.

For some reason I've never been able to fade into the background. I attract scrutiny. I open my mouth and defences go up. Alarms go off. Jean says I need to be more flexible, I need to learn to intrude less when my dream world interfaces with someone else's. This is where she loses me. What we experience, she says, is nothing more than the dream of God. Or gods. Eastern mumbo jumbo, but it works for her. I've learned to shut her out whenever she talks this way. But perhaps I should heed her advice, because here was another situation where I should have held my tongue. I leaned forward in my seat and buried my face in my hands. I felt powerless. I could feel a headache coming on, a throbbing pain right behind my eyes.

This customs woman had something against us, plain and simple. Her movements were deliberately slow, as if our sole purpose in being there was to move through her world like the hands of a clock, measuring and giving shape to her day. Something was stuck in her craw. She ran our names through her computer and even though nothing showed up, I sensed she doubted what she saw. We had to be on somebody's wanted list. We had that criminal look about us. Just her doubts made me feel caged. As I say, I could read reproach in her eyes. After four days on the road, though, we must have appeared seedy, I had to give her that. Eric looked like he'd slept in his clothes, and the part Jean had so painstakingly combed into his hair from the day he started kindergarten had been replaced by an unruly mop. And after three straight late nights of heavy drinking, Jamie had black circles ringing his puffy eyes. To add to this portrait, Gus and I already sported the beginnings of patchy beards. Maybe she thought we'd stolen the passports. Who knows?

I sat up, leaned back in my chair and locked my hands behind my head. I watched her move behind her counter. I tried drawing in long breaths through my nose and exhaling through my mouth. I turned my head from side to side, but my neck and shoulder muscles were tight. Twice I caught her looking at me. I wondered, If I were able to see past the uniform, past the delay, would my judgment be different? Would I care that her skin was too pale, her nose crooked? Would she be someone I would want to know? Or the flip side? Would I be someone she would want to know?

When a message arrived from the British Consulate back in Washington, she acted as if nothing had happened, as if everything were as right as rain. She stamped Jamie's passport and waved us on our way. She laughed at something Gus said, patted Eric on the head, but made no apology. Nothing. And then, as if answering the look I gave her, she wished us a safe journey and said she was just doing her job. Her eyes were radiant and, in a curious gesture as we walked out, she let her hair down to tumble freely about her shoulders.

Nice woman, Gus said, but man o man, I wouldn't want her job, not for all the money in the world. Too many miserable sons of bitches, too many geeks, to have to deal with. And he laughed.

As we pulled away from the building, the Stars and Stripes flapping in the breeze, all I could think was that I was grateful we had survived our ordeal. At long last we were liberated spirits on our way south, turnpike bound, to sip the narcotic of golden dreams and to wallow in the great sun-splashed free-for-all that is America.

For Gus and Jamie, the appeal of the journey was simply in being on the road, with no responsibilities, to see how many states we could visit in thirteen days. I felt a certain responsibility to watch my daughter play in at least one soccer game, while Eric was happy to be going places where his older sister had never been. Shelley had flown to Minneapolis with Jean and would not see any of the country between. I also saw this expedition as an opportunity for Eric and me to spend some time together, free from the influence of the women in our lives. Without intending any disrespect, although God knows all sorts of people will interpret what I'm about to say in the wrong way, I felt Eric was too much a mother's boy. For the first four years of his life he'd clung to his mother like a barnacle to rock. At night he'd only sleep clinging to her stomach.

It's because of his colic, Jean had explained.

Because he's jealous, I'd thought of answering back, but didn't, knowing this would have led to unnecessary recrimination.

From the age of six on he showed he could be stubbornly independent, but if he was in trouble, he ran to the sheltering skirts of his mother. He'd already divined who was his ally. Who was most likely to scold, hug and forget. Undoubtedly most people will think I was at least partly to blame for this, although throughout the summer months Eric and I played catch in the back yard, between the vegetable garden and the grape arbour, in amongst the apple, plum and cherry trees. We worked on grounders and fly balls. But it was true, I'd never taken charge or given advice. I saw this trip as an opportunity to confide in him, to tell him those things my father had been unable to tell me. Eric seemed too young for a serious discussion about sex, but Jean kept hounding me, kept asking me if I'd had *my* talk with *my* son yet. That took gall, talking as if she had nothing to do with the process. When I protested she said, They get older younger these days, Rob. They grow up so quickly, she said. Say something to him. For God's sake, just say *something*, she said quietly, before it's too late. Before he knows more than we do!

What makes you think he doesn't already know more than we do, I thought of asking, a not-so-clever reply, and one certain to precipitate further discord.

This was the subject of discussion the evening before her departure. Sprawled across the bed, I sipped a glass of port and puffed on a small Dutch cigar while

Jean packed her suitcase. She folded everything with a neatness I felt bordered on obsession. This was typical of Jean. Not a hair out of place.

You're only going for twelve days, I said. And as soon as you arrive you have to unpack. What's the point of all this?

I felt like reaching in and scrambling the whole mess together.

Don't even think it, she said and raised an eyebrow. She placed a magazine and her weekly cryptic cross-word puzzle on top. You packed yet?

I shook my head.

Try not to leave it till the last minute this time, Rob. She closed the lid and snapped the clasps together. And don't forget you'll have to pack for Eric as well. She had that smug look about her that she got when she thought I couldn't take care of myself.

She seemed to have some sort of cataclysm in mind that I couldn't fathom. She looked at me as if I were incapable of grasping the importance of what she was saying, as if a part of me were undeveloped, as if that part had, by some miracle, survived in a foetal state, without a whisper of conscience. She gazed at me as if I were guilty for the hair she imagined was growing out of Eric's palms. Clearly she would hold me responsible when his dick dropped off moments after he was in-fected by a toilet seat.

At best, it seemed to me, I ranked up there with all the other social misfits of the last millennium: oddballs such as the Marquis de Sade, Rasputin, Wilde, Sadam.

You and Eric will have a wonderful time, she said,

moving her case off the bed and out into the hallway. A bus was to pick up Shelley and her at three in the morning for the long haul to Seattle where they'd catch a direct flight to the twin cities. I know you will, she said.

I stubbed out the cigar and rolled over onto my back. With this vote of confidence, I couldn't possibly tell her how nervous the whole damn trip made me feel.

As I see it, and this is how I would explain myself if Jean were to ask: When the sun rises there has to be someone willing to take the blame—where there's cause—for yesterday. For what didn't happen. For what wasn't said. I'll admit I'm the silent type, my feelings guarded, while Jean is what other people call forthright. Nothing embarrasses her. What I reckon is, she takes a perverse delight in watching me squirm. In her mind, as she repeatedly tells me, I'm never there when she really needs me, not in the moments that count, as in this matter of Eric's passage through puberty into adulthood. In the weeks leading up to our departure, this complaint had become more vociferous. I was then and am now tempted to tell her that I can't be everywhere at once, that I'm not the deity she thought I was when we married, but I'm sure she'd come back at me with, It would be good to find you somewhere, anywhere outside the boundaries, the limits of your own mind. Your own ego. She would not mean to be harsh, her comments likely followed by a kiss, my senses drugged on her perfume and soft skin.

A wonderful time, she said, setting the alarm and turning off the bedside light.

Her two favourite occasions for telling me I need to be a better father are at breakfast when I'm drinking my coffee and reading the local newspaper and just after she pops a sleeping pill and is waiting for darkness to descend, for her lids to close on the day. I see these monologues as a kind of purging before the purity of dream. She tells me I'm rarely in her dreams, and, when I am, I'm usually only cast in the role of guest.

Could it ever be otherwise? I ask.

From the moment we arrived in the Twin Cities, Jean seemed upset because we four 'boys' had rented a couple of motel rooms with air conditioning. She saw no reason why we shouldn't suffer as much as she was. She was stuck in university dorms as a chaperone for a group of teenage girls. And the nineteen-year-old boys from New York city, lodged on the same floor and hyped on testosterone, were more than she cared to control. They were all over our girls, she said. Into the early hours of the morning she was certain she heard movement throughout the old brick building. I tried to imagine Jean patrolling the halls, leaping out of the shadows to catch a young couple in mid clutch.

On our way into the city I had noticed black thunderheads forming from the clouds that swirled above the lakes. Minneapolis was hot and humid, and Jean had tossed and turned through thunderstorms every night since she and the girls had arrived. She hadn't slept, she said, not since she'd left home.

After watching two soccer games played on fields

planted over peat, the ball bouncing as if gravity were an afterthought, and with a hot prairie wind whirling around our heads, Jean said she needed a breather. She wanted to go back to our motel, take a lengthy shower and then lounge in the luxury of the air conditioning. I could mix the drinks. Eric could spend the afternoon with Gus and Jamie.

We were standing inside a large building the size of two football fields, the only spot out of the sun in a few miles' radius. Dozens of kids in soccer boots, shorts, and brightly coloured jerseys milled around booths and wolfed down hotdogs, hamburgers and pop. A recording of Arrowsmith had just finished and the lyrics "Your crime is time and its/18 and life to go" by Skid Row bounced off the walls while someone gave a running commentary over the PA system on souvenirs for sale— sweat shirts, t-shirts, mugs, pennants, posters, pins. Our girls were lost somewhere in this zoo. I jumped up and down a couple of times to see if I could see Shelley and then bent towards Jean.

This is supposed to be our time together, Eric's and mine, I said. You were the one who suggested the trip in the first place.

Shelley suddenly appeared a few feet in front of us, holding up a sweat shirt with a soccer ball zooming above the words, *Minnesota: Home of the U.S.A. Cup.* The names of several participating countries formed a puzzle of sorts in the trail left by the ball. She struck a pose, her face filled with happiness.

A few hours won't hurt, Jean said—and she stopped as if considering her words more carefully—won't make any difference to the bonding process. The tone of her voice, her sarcasm, pissed me off. I felt she had already judged the trip a failure, but then she reached up, tipped my chin towards her, looked into my eyes and said, I'm sorry Rob, I was kidding.

I turned back and saw Shelley's lips mouthing, asking, Well, can I have it? I nodded. Immediately she disappeared back into the crowd. And briefly, for the first time, I saw Jean's high cheek bones, long legs and small hips in the fleeting image of our daughter. Her blossoming womanish beauty. I marvelled that this lithe creature who moved magically, like a shadow of sorts, in and out of my life, was actually my flesh and blood. Jean's mother, who took delight in puncturing these moments with her own special view of history, would say, One good romp in the hay can play havoc with the best of family trees.

I have no idea why I persisted, except I wanted Jean to know how I felt. I wanted her to understand that I lacked the sort of control she seemed to have over her feelings. That sometimes I got tired of being reminded of how useless I could be. I stared out through the two large doors at the dust eddies kicked up by the wind.

Do you remember what you said? I asked. Back when you volunteered me for this reclamation project. You said, This will provide a wonderful opportunity for the two of you to get to know each other better. As I say, your words. Verbatim. I looked up at the massive steel girders that supported the roof. I remember thinking the place was like a giant echo chamber in which every word would eventually be heard by everyone else in the building. I lowered my voice and said, So far I don't think it's worked. He hardly knows I'm alive. He has more of a rapport with Gus, for Christ's sake.

Rob. Not now, all right.

She pushed her fingers through her hair and poked the toe of her sandal at the cement floor. I want to go with you to the motel. Alone. Just the two of us. Okay? She looked at me, one eye casting slightly to the side, as it did when she sensed I wasn't paying attention. Do you hear what I'm saying?

I did, but I wasn't sure I wanted to. Why I felt this way I wasn't sure, either, except I knew pride can kill both desire and pleasure. I wanted to tell her what was on my mind—that sometimes when she carried on, when she talked too freely, I felt embarrassed. Compromised. And yet, I also admired the way in which she could be carefree, intimate, not necessarily under obligation.

A voice on the loudspeaker began to announce bus departures and suddenly we were a still point in a flow of swarming colours.

Don't you think we should ask Gus first? I said. I mean he's just spent half a day watching teenage girls boot a ball around a cow pasture. Maybe he has other plans.

She shifted her weight on to her toes, placed both hands on my chest and pressed up against me, her breath hot on my face. Then I could feel her knee push into my groin, gently moving back and forth.

It wasn't that bad, she said. I thought they played quite well. This wasn't that much of a hardship, especially for Gus. I think he always finds some little pleasure in the movements of the female form.

I started to protest—after all, this was our daughter we were speaking of—and she stepped back, crossed her arms and glanced at the floor. The building was empty except for the people closing down the booths. Shaking her head, she said, Jesus, Rob, sometimes I wonder. I really do. Standing in front of me, dressed in white shorts, a fuchsia-coloured blouse and leather sandals, her whole body seemed to glow, to invite me to breathe her in. She stood perfectly still and her voice went quiet, sounding almost vulnerable, spellbinding. Anyway, you'll all be back on your own tomorrow. Then she walked past me, out into the sunlight.

When I found Gus and told him what Jean wanted, he winked and said, I'd have been surprised if you hadn't asked me to look after the sprout for at least a couple of hours. Take as long as you need. Don't rush things on our account. And he put his arm around my shoulder and pulled me towards him, All the time it takes, you understand. Then he gave me a small push and punch on the shoulder and laughed.

This man-to-man machismo was not what I needed at that moment. Gus's mouth had widened until his ears, eyes, nose, chin, cheeks, forehead seemed to disappear behind an enormous set of conspiratorial lips. For an uneasy few moments, we stood side by side, wordless, until I winked and he seemed satisfied we had an agreement. To be honest, I didn't know what I wanted. What I did know was that I was filled with uncertainty, which was not something I remembered feeling before, or something that I could or wanted to talk to Gus about. Most of the time, men can't talk to each other freely, not about their feelings, especially not to someone like Gus.

We rounded up and loaded the girls onto the bus returning back to the dorms, and the four of us plus Jean piled into the Volvo wagon and headed downtown. In a shopping section of St. Paul, Gus asked that the three of them be let off.

Are you sure you don't mind? I asked, pushing my head out the window.

Don't give us another thought, he said.

We won't, Jean interrupted and smiled, her fingernails digging into my arm.

Gus gave a little shrug and chuckled. The three of us'll walk back to the motel from here. He looked around, as if he knew where he was. Can't be more than two or three miles. I'm sure I recognize some of the buildings. He glanced up and motioned with his hand at the brick facades that lined both sides of the street. We'll see you two lovebirds in a few hours.

Jamie nodded and Eric looked pleased, as if he were part of a conspiracy. I knew he was happy to be roaming and exploring the streets of a city he'd only seen before on TV, the home of the Twins and Vikings.

The moment I closed the door of the motel room, Jean turned and faced me. She unbuttoned her blouse, unfastened her bra and said, I need air. I need to cool off, Rob. My skin needs to breathe. It's so damp and warm out there. So close. Then she slid her shorts down and stepped out of them. From her shoulder bag she removed a bottle of lotion she smoothed over her skin, careful not to miss any crease she could reach. Her body glistened.

And I just stood there dumbfounded, surprised by how good she looked. By how firm her body was, at how sleek and supple she appeared. Her hands caressed her breasts and she said, Don't be bashful, Rob, we're alone, in case you hadn't noticed!

I *had* noticed and I wanted her, but I felt awkward and clumsy, like I was shadow without a form to attach to.

When I moved towards her, she said, You get the spots I missed, okay? She turned away from me and lifted and held her hair bunched on top of her head. I spread the liquid on my fingers and slowly rotated my hand across her shoulders, circling and circling, down to the small of her back. When I started to knead her hips with both hands, she slipped her panties down and let them fall to the floor.

For some inexplicable reason I hesitated and she spun about to face me, wrapped one leg around mine and slowly, gently, rubbed her hips and breasts against me. Then she began to unfasten my belt. How long has it been anyway? Since we were really, really alone? And together? she added. No responsibilities. No housework. Unattached. She spoke quietly. You know what surprises me the most, she said, about being away from home?

She pinched my chin between her thumb and forefinger and looked into my eyes, her expression challenging. For a moment, from somewhere deep inside her body, she was talking to me. I sensed a need she had to be wanted. To be desirable. To be loved.

I don't feel as though I have to account for myself, she said. For what I'm thinking, or what I do. I like that, don't you?

The curtained room was dark, but I tensed up with each sound that penetrated the walls from the noisy street outside—cars, trucks, a radio, someone running, the rhythmic swishing of a broom.

I guess I looked uneasy, distracted, because Jean pushed me onto the bed, placed one hand at the back of my head and ruffled my hair. The other hand she slid between my legs, and then she whispered, What I'm saying, Rob, is that I want to spend the afternoon making love. Uninterrupted.

There was a time when this is what we lived for, I said. The hopes we had.

She nodded, placing the tip of a finger on my lips.

I caught hold of her hand and interlocked our fingers. A beam of sunlight cut through a slit in the curtains and reflected off the wall mirror. Sparkling.

Then anything was possible, I continued. Like that first afternoon we spent at the beach, talking about all the places we would travel to, places we would share. Paris, Rome, Bombay, Bali. Talking about our senses. Talking about how we both wanted to taste everything the world had to offer. Me boasting about walking through the mountains from San Sebastion to Madrid, smelling the dust and dry heat of the high plateau, drinking wine in a tapas bar, how surprised I was by its earthen floor, about meeting a quiet, gentle man who

194

claimed to be a bullfighter and doubting him, later seeing his face on posters in Seville. You pulling me and my stories into you through your pores, with each breath, with each blink of your eyes. Like camera shutters. Both of us burning inside, between our thighs, in the palms of our hands.

Like pieris blooming in spring, I had thought.

The street noises subsided and the only sound we could hear was the music of a band coming from the direction of the alley that ran behind the motel.

When I entered her, she said, Whoa. Slow down, Rob. We have nothing but time, okay, nothing but time. She stopped moving, rolled over on top and looked down at me. The muscles in her face were taut, her eyes imploring. I want you to move slowly, make it last. I want you to remember who we are, without regret. She bent forward and kissed me. Make it last, she said. As if we have forever. Please.

In the darkness, Jean sleeping beside me, I wonder, Is this what we lose as we get older, our sense of urgency and anticipation, placed on hold, becalmed by our willingness to compromise? By our concern to do what we hope is the right thing?

As we got ready to go to the ball game between the Twins and Yankees at the Metrodome, I sat on the end of the bed and watched Jean pull my hairbrush through the long, wet strands of her hair. Eric had come to the room half an hour earlier, expecting us to be dressed. When he peered into the room and saw us both wrapped in towels, he looked as if he'd been betrayed. For a moment he stood in the doorway, the fingers of his right hand playing with his lower lip. He stared at the floor, at his feet, pigeon-toed, then turned and left without closing the door. He had resisted us, had resisted running into the room, probably to Jean, to seek reassurance. As she came back to the bed, Jean said he seemed like a kid who was a little bit frightened, a slightly pudgy blond kid, caught in one of those stages of growth where he seemed not quite human, who'd had a scare, as if he'd just seen his parents slip back to a time that didn't include him. Now we were going to be late, at least for batting practice and the pre-game show.

I looked at Jean's long legs, one crossed over the other. Her face was lost behind hair that flew away from the hairdryer. I had to remind myself that only an hour ago we had held each other, tightly, each breathing in the scent of the other. Each tonguing the other's skin. I had to remind myself that we had shared a passion that I believed had long ago disappeared from our lives. From our marriage. Lying side by side on the bed, I had wanted to tell her I felt I'd come as close to death as I thought possible. That I had this sensation of not being. But I didn't think this would make much sense to her, as it didn't to me. It was just a feeling I had. So I kissed her, lay back and said nothing.

We arrived too late for batting practice and Eric was clearly disappointed because several of the girls, including his sister, had managed to scramble after balls hit into the left-field bleachers. As soon as the game got under way and he saw a vacant seat beside his mother, he went and sat with her. She put her arm around him and pulled him towards her. As I watched them, I realized how comfortable he felt in her company. And I figured he probably blamed me because he didn't have a ball.

The game was not exciting. I think the final score was six to one for the Yankees, although I'm not certain because in the fifth inning I strolled out into the concourse and bought a signed ball from one of the vendors. He was a large black man who seemed more interested in reminiscing about a game played thirty years ago than in watching the game being played that night. I told him this was not a ballpark like the ones I had envisioned as a kid listening to the World Series games played between Brooklyn and New York. Ebbet's Field, he said, you'd be speaking of Ebbet's Field. He'd grown up within spitting distance of Ebbet's Field. Now that was a ballpark. No astro turf. No roof. It isn't the players' fault, he said, most of them still love the game. Playing baseball indoors, he said, is like having sex with a rubber doll. He laughed. Bounces are true and always predictable, he added. No style, no skill, no feel.

When I gave Eric the ball on the way out of the stadium, he turned it round and round, as though spinning and exploring a previously unexplored planet, until he found Kirby Puckett's name. Kirby was special. Eric ran up to his sister and stuck it in her face. She showed it to her friends and then looked at me and smiled. I knew she was pleased for him.

Jean herded the girls onto a bus. She looked miserable as she followed them up the stairs, each step so laboured she might have been gasping for oxygen at the summit of some previously unclimbed mountain in the Himalayas. At the top she turned and waved, then lifted her hand and blew us a kiss.

Eric said, Did you see what Mum did?

I nodded.

We left the dome at around eleven and walked west, away from the Mississippi, away from our motel, into the commercial centre of the city. We were surrounded by shopping malls and concrete towers filled with reflecting black glass. High up in the towers, lit windows appeared as though hung like film negatives, detached, in space. The streets were deserted except for the occasional cab whose movements seemed furtive.

I get the feeling we're not supposed to be here at this hour, Gus said. The whole damn place is shut down. Like some sort of dead zone.

Jamie had moved ahead of us and was taking photographs. Even if we hadn't been able to see his shadowy figure, we'd have been able to follow his movements from the small flash of light that blinked with each shot. Then he disappeared around a corner.

Stupid bloody fool'll get himself mugged, Gus said.

We ran ahead and came onto a large open area, acres and acres of asphalt with tufts of weed and grass growing up between the cracks, and signs posted every hundred feet or so that said "Reserved Parking." And out in the middle a lone cop car sat, away from the orange street lights. Jamie was already moving towards it, his camera aimed.

198

His camera flashed.

Perfect, he called back to us. Just let me get one more shot, up close. My mates'll love this.

As he crouched and adjusted the focus, a spotlight lit up the whole area and a voice said, What the hell's going on out there?

Jamie stood up, lifted his hand to shade his eyes and said, Sorry. Didn't realize anyone was in there. Would you mind if I took a photograph of you and your car?

The spotlight went out and Jamie took this gesture to mean he'd been given approval to go ahead. He bent forward and once again aimed his camera. From what I could see, I thought the cop was about to say no, but just then the flash went off. At the same time, a woman's head popped up, smiling, in the window. As quickly the cop pushed her back down, out of view. For the moment he had a bemused look on his face.

Gus said, Perfect timing! Jesus Christ, Jamie. He looked at the cop and smiled. We're out of here. Nice to meet you, he said, glancing back—half expecting to see a gun pointing after us, he told me later.

What's he doing to her? Eric asked.

Jamie, winding his film, saying thank you, started to move towards the car. I grabbed him by the sleeve and pulled him after Gus and Eric towards the main street.

It's not so much what he's doing to her as what she's doing for him, Gus said. He had Eric under the shoulder and lifted him as he half walked, half ran, away.

What do you mean? Eric said, struggling to get free, to make contact with the ground.

I wanted to tell Gus to let Eric alone, that my kid could make it on his own, without his help, that Eric had watched enough TV to have acquired some street savvy, but my own tussle with Jamie suggested otherwise. He and I looked like we were dancing a frantic waltz across the parking lot, moving in large loops as he tried to turn back towards the cop car and I tried to steer him in the opposite direction.

We'll talk later, Gus said to Eric, Now I think it's best we make our way back in the direction of the motel. As quickly as possible.

When we reached the lighted street, Jamie said, Did you see the expression on that copper's face? Priceless, he said. And hers! There's got to be a prize-winning photo or magazine cover in that picture. I realized then that he didn't have a clue what was happening when he was taking the photograph. Gus was right, we could have got ourselves seriously injured. Shot seemed as likely a possibility.

As my eyes begin to adjust to the darkness, I want to laugh when I think about Ford's story "Winterkill," when Les says, "Trouble comes cheap and leaves expensive." I want to be glib and say, Ain't that the truth, but sometimes there's a fine line between what some people call desperation and what others see as honesty, as the inevitable working out of things. I don't imagine that cop had given too much thought to his actions. To the next song he'd sing or the colours he'd gaze on in tomorrow's sunrise, from radiant yellow to orange to green to shadows flirting in an alley. We do what we can to break away from routine, from the monotony of things.

The next morning we packed the Volvo and drove up to the university to say our goodbyes. Jean took my hand, squeezed it, and said, Thanks. I must have looked puzzled. For yesterday, she said. I looked away, embarrassed that Gus or Jamie might see, that everyone there, the players and coaches, would know what had happened the day before. But they were too busy getting ready to head off to the field. Bags were being counted and stuffed into the bus. Somebody had forgotten their shin guards. I wanted to tell Jean about what we'd seen after the game, in the early hours of the morning. I don't know why. Maybe I thought it would excite her. In a strange way I envied the cop and the woman he'd been with for the risk they were taking. For the ease with which they'd accepted our bungling interruption. Or maybe he was just too flustered, too stunned, to say anything, as I would have been. Such a small thing can cut a huge hole in your life.

Missouri. Just the name sounded like we'd crossed some invisible line into the south. In my imagination this was the land of live and let live. Masks and shrimp boats. Parades and poker. Contradictions. This was what I imagined. Cats, stray cats, and hounds, howling at the moon rising over the river. And heavy, dead air. Explosive air, air worked up into a frenzy, air that became tornadoes or hurricanes. I imagined soft horns and banjos, voices that sang like silk. Kerchiefs and bowler hats.

Butterflies and magnolia trees. And churches, churches filled with God-fearing folk.

On the outskirts of Kansas City, we stopped at a place called the Red Lion Inn. After checking into our rooms, we made our way to the restaurant. Jamie said he had a craving for a large steak and lobster and a Caesar salad.

I'll buy the wine, Gus said. Something to go with a blue steak. I had no idea I was so hungry.

Led by a man dressed in tails and a red bow tie, we wound through families seated at tables covered with white linen and silver to one of several large booths backing on to an outside wall and elevated on a platform a step up from the main dining area. I couldn't for the life of me figure out if the maitre d' was trying to hide us or place us on exhibit. As I looked around the room, what surprised me was that all the men were wearing dark suits or jackets and ties and the women were decked out in dresses, formal and drab. Even the kids were dressed up.

Jamie frowned as we sat down. I have to say, he said, I feel a tad uncomfortable. He fingered his cotton shirt and jeans. I think we're slightly underdressed. Feel like I'm at a bloody banker's convention. He took a sip from his iced water and screwed up his face. What we need is a serious drink. A single malt's just what the doctor ordered. He patted down his hair and waved his arm, trying to catch the attention of one of the waiters who zigzagged back and forth across the room below us.

It's Sunday, I said. I'd forgotten what day it was. These people have probably just come from church. Or maybe it's the custom in this part of the country to go out for a Sunday meal. I don't know. But we must look like one hell of a crew, I whispered.

How do they dress like that in this heat? Gus said, a bit too loudly for my liking. Anyway, these bible belters'll have to take us as we are. You know what they say. You can't change a leopard's spots. He settled back to read the menu.

When I glanced up, I could see that most heads were bent over plates of food, but every so often someone looked up at us, sized us up, and then said something to others at their table, which added to the low murmurs that whirred around the room in time with the hum of several ceiling fans. Nothing distinct. Only suspicions.

When the waiter came to take our orders, Jamie and I ordered steaks, medium-rare, and Eric asked if he could have a hamburger.

No, I said, order something off the menu. You like pasta. Have lasagna. You can't always be eating hamburgers. Besides, lasagna is the Italian equivalent of a hamburger. Okay?

No. I want a burger, Eric insisted.

We don't serve hamburgers, sir, the waiter said.

Have you got buns? Gus asked.

We have rolls, the waiter replied.

Are they large enough to hold a patty of meat?

I imagine so.

Well, then, Gus said, grind up a steak, grill it, put it in a bun and give the kid what he wants. I'll have a ten-ounce steak, blue. You know what that means?

Yes sir, the waiter said and sighed.

You sure?

Yes sir.

The waiter turned and left.

What's blue, Eric asked.

The only way to eat a steak, Gus said. Anything else is a violation. He looked to the next table, making sure he could be heard. Blue is when they take your steak, at least one inch thick, sizzle it for ten seconds on either side at five hundred degrees. He shut his eyes and ran his tongue along his lips. The outside is singed, the inside is still alive.

Now he looked at Jamie and said, So Jamie, do you know the difference between a hooker, a mistress and a wife?

I don't, Jamie said, but I'm sure I'm about to find out.

Well, Gus said, the hooker says, Are you done yet? The mistress says, Are you done already? And the wife, filled with the romance of the moment, says, and here he paused for effect, Beige. I think we should paint the ceiling beige. Gus laughed.

Got it, Jamie said, smiling but not laughing. This time you won't have to explain it to me. He lifted his drink, shook his head and then winked at Eric. And the lesson is? He hesitated, but not long enough to give Gus a chance to reply. I assume there is a lesson! He emptied his glass.

Do you miss her? Your girl back home? Back in England? Gus asked, as he tucked his napkin into the front of his shirt.

Jamie messed his hair with both hands. No, he said, not really. But that's not what you want to hear, is it Gus?

For the past six days, ever since Jamie had inadvertently mentioned he had a girlfriend back home, Gus had been on his case.

So when's the big day? Gus said.

Jamie shrugged his shoulders and raised his eyebrows, as if he didn't have the slightest idea what Gus was talking about.

The wedding? When are the two of you getting hitched?

It's not that sort of relationship, Jamie said.

And what sort is it? Gus said.

We live together, Gus, it's not a big deal, Jamie said. We co-habit, is that the word? Okay? He took a deep breath and studied Gus's face. All right, I confess, we live in sin. Does that make you happy?

Why should it make him happy? Eric said. He had been listening to their conversation intensely, but I could see he was still trying to follow its path.

Because I'm not married, Jamie said. That seems to excite the old fella. Gus, I mean. He gets to thinking about lost prospects. He's envious. That's what he is, jealous. Now do you understand?

I think so, Eric said.

So, Gus said, it's like that, is it? He smiled. You should be ashamed of yourself. You should do the honourable thing and marry the girl.

Bouncing up and down in his seat, Eric said, Not like Karen, eh Gus? If it were your daughter, she'd be getting married at the business end of a shotgun.

He said this loudly enough so that people at other tables turned to look at us. A couple of heads wagged back and forth.

Gus, taking Eric's words in stride, made a gun with his hand, pointed it at him, and pulled the trigger. You got me, Eric, he said, fair and square, right between the eyes.

I looked at Eric and said, Where the hell did that come from? Where'd you pick up that notion.

Yesterday, he said, when Gus and I were watching cartoons. When we were waiting for you and mum. Before we went to the ball game. Why? What's wrong with what I said?

Nothing, I said.

The woman at the next table shook her head and watched me. The way she looked at me made me feel naked, as if there was nothing to me. I resented whatever it was she expected.

Nothing at all, I repeated. Just keep your voice down.

The woman, whose face was now pink and pinched like a rosebud, stood up, took her daughter by the hand and retreated to the lobby. Her husband paid the bill, slipped a tip under his saucer, and then turned towards us. His mouth moved without sound, like a fish under water, but before he could leave, I mouthed back, Fuck you, too.

I don't know why I did that.

Just before sunset, as we walked back to our rooms, I heard a train whistle, a sound that could be comforting or forlorn, depending on your mood. The sky turned from grey and crimson to dull grey and then grew darker. Leaden. The air was heavy with the anticipation of rain.

On the slow climb towards Topeka, rain pelting the

windshield, we got stuck behind a truck with a large camper on the back. The vehicle swayed and swerved as winds buffeted the unit from both sides. When we came to a passing lane, I pulled out, but when we got along-side, Gus told me to slow down, to pull in behind again. He wanted to read the sticker stuck to the camper door.

Get closer, he said.

I cut back in behind the truck, so close the windshield flooded and we were driving blind. I braked and turned up the wipers. Gus leaned forward and read through the back-and-forth whip of the blades. Stay . . . free . . . mini . . . pad, he stuttered. Thought that's what it said. Good one, and Gus, Jamie and I laughed.

What's so funny? Eric asked.

Nothing, I said.

Come on, he said, you're not laughing at nothing.

You wouldn't understand, I said. Right away I regret-ted saying that.

Eric kicked the back of my seat.

We often laugh at nothing, Gus said. Eric kicked his seat. Did you read the sticker?

No, Eric said.

Just as well, I said, trying to catch Gus's attention.

But Gus was too slow to put a clamp on it. Well, it said "Stay Free Mini Pad." Do you know what that is? he asked.

Sort of, Eric said.

And what would that be, Gus continued.

In the rear view mirror I could see Eric glance at Jamie. Then he poked him, but Jamie continued to look out the side window at the farm fields.

Ask Jamie, Eric said, see if he knows.

I remembered Jean telling me about the time Eric had busted into the bathroom when she was taking a bath. She'd left a tampon sitting on the counter by the sink. Eric, who was five said, Sorry, 'scuse me, pulled down his fly, pissed, stared down at Jean in the bathtub, said nothing, appeared to notice nothing, flushed, and wheeled around to leave. Then he caught sight of the tampon. What's that? he asked. Jean had been hoping he'd depart in the same blur he'd entered and wouldn't notice. A tampon, she said. Eric glanced back at her and said, Oh, ugh, I tried one of those once, tasted awful, and sped out the door.

At that moment, out there on the highway, in the rain, I'd have been just as happy if the skies had cleared, the sun had shone, and the camper, with its sticker, and wherever this lesson was leading, could be wiped from the face of the earth. But I could see Eric still jabbing Jamie, only now a little more vigorously.

Finally Jamie said, Pad, you know what a pad is?

Yeah.

What?

You tell me, Eric said.

Well, pad is a name for a place where you live. Like a flat.

Or an apartment, I said.

I knew that, Eric said.

So a mini pad would be a small apartment, Jamie said.

And "stay free" means the guy driving that camper doesn't have to pay, Gus added. He has his home on wheels. See, it's simple. He turned in his seat and looked back at Eric. That's what we were laughing at.

Eric stared back at him. No, he said, there's something else. There's something you're not telling me. You guys wouldn't have made a big deal out of that.

What I didn't anticipate was how badly Gus and I would screw up trying to explain female anatomy and physiology to Eric. Or that Eric would ask so many questions. I wondered if this leg of the trip resembled the sort of rituals the Indians put their boys through. Where they deprived them of oxygen so they would have hallucinations. That's what we needed. A sweat lodge, not a Volvo wagon. And a hallucination or two.

Jamie was as good as useless. Midway through this exchange, somewhere on the I-70, just outside of Denver, I realized he was just as mystified by our descriptions and explanations as Eric was. Now, as I think about it, I'm not sure anything Gus or I said bore any resemblance to reality.

At least the rain had let up.

When Gus launched into details about a woman's period, about lunar movements and cycles, and made some wisecrack about howling dogs, I knew we were in trouble. When I said a pad was placed between a woman's legs to absorb blood—that it was more like a sponge than a Band Aid because a woman couldn't stop the bleeding—that this bleeding happened for a few days each month, Gus leapt in and asked if Eric had noticed that his mum got crabby at the same time every month—or that she got forgetful and unreasonable— or that she got tired, of you and your dad—or that your dad got this hungry look on his face, like something was missing from his life—well, it was then I realized we'd lost sight of land, that we were soaring through outer space without a compass.

And, Gus said, Stay Free is a brand name for one of those pads we've been talking about.

Oh, Eric said.

Gus rubbed his forehead and shrugged.

So it was a pun, I said. The sticker was a pun. Back on the truck we saw, the sticker was a pun. Not a particularly good pun. I'm sorry now Gus pointed it out.

I think I get it, Eric said. But I was pretty certain he didn't. I wanted to tell him that I didn't think men understood much, not about pain or patience, both of which had a lot to do with sex and the body, so whether he got the pun or not didn't matter. We were after something more basic here.

But why do they have to bleed? Eric said. It's cruel.

I thought for a moment he was going to cry, but he didn't.

He said, It's cruel they have to do that every month.

Gus and I stared ahead, towards the sunset that appeared below the cloud layer that hung over the city— a thin line of orange and aqua green. I knew both of us felt this was a conversation we wished we'd never started. I felt like I'd been caught up in a lie out of control—a lie that says you're still single, ignorant and consequences are not only predictable but acceptable.

We left Cheyenne and made the gradual ascent to the high plains of Wyoming. Before us stretched miles of barbed wire fence, range, tumbleweed and a few scrappy-looking pines. Wide open spaces. Occasionally we saw what we figured had been homesteads or line cabins of some sort. Abandoned. In one sense, I thought, this was country you could wrap around yourself, get lost in. A huge threadbare coat of a country, where the heartbeat beneath was the pulse of the earth itself. I sensed a breathing so close, I felt spooked. But if you could part with most creature comforts and could follow the dreaming mind where it took you, then this would be a great place to live. For most people, though, this would be a place of monotonous rolling hills, an empty place on a road leading to somewhere hospitable. Somewhere with hot water, a soft bed, and another soft body. Even so this was a place where you could and would most likely be alone. There was a strange and alluring appeal in that, I thought. I glanced in the mirror and saw that Eric and Jamie were asleep. From the corner of my eye I could see Gus squinting, looking into the distance in much the same way he did when we were out fishing. He was quiet, motionless. Listening.

All that sky, he said softly. No clouds even. Nothing to hold on to. This is the sort of place that makes me long for the love of a woman and a warm bed.

We descended into Rock Springs in early evening, the sun dropping across the way, behind the hills to the west. Below us a city spread out. I don't remember it as desert, all I remember is dirt and rock, a place that appeared to be a permanent construction site. Every-

thing—buildings, roads, mines, mobile homes, vegetation—looked temporary. Jamie, who had been asleep
the last few hours, his head stuffed into a couple of
pillows he'd swiped from our night in Cheyenne,
rubbed his eyes with his fists and said, Bloody hell,
where have you brought me?

Gus turned and said, Look who's awake! Alive even.
We gave you up for dead miles back. You should feel
right at home in this place.

We took a main road off the highway to a motel
called Western Skies, a two-storey structure which
looked out on a central parking lot. There were no flowers or trees, no grass—nothing. Asphalt bled into dirt.
A red and black neon sign blinked against the blacken-
ing sky.

As we walked from the office to our rooms, Gus said,
I need a beer after breathing in goddamn dust all day,
and Jamie looks like he needs the cure. A little hair of the
dog. But I warn you, he said to me, this kid's a menace.

You're an old man, Gus, Jamie said. You've got no
stamina. At the bar last night, he said, glancing at me,
there were all these women looking for dancing partners and what does the old guy do, he seeks out the
only woman in the state of Wyoming who knows a
cousin of a cousin of hers whose aunt knows Gus's wife's
brother-in-law's sister who says he's reputed to be hap-
pily married, and they slink off into a corner to discuss
fidelity, or mutual acquaintances, or some such rubbish, leaving me alone to entertain the ladies. Mind
you, I'm not complaining.

As we neared our rooms, the streetlights came on

and the last tinges of orange disappeared from the sky. Eric ran ahead and unlocked the doors.

Unbelievable, Gus said, a pensive look on his face. I travel five thousand miles into the heartland of North America, I finally get up the courage to talk to a woman in a small bar in the remotest state of the Union, I'm finally willing to take a risk because this woman turns me on, and within five minutes I find out she knows my wife. Knows Claire for Christ's sake. What're the odds?

Finally, I said, a little miffed. An edge of sarcasm crept into my voice. What's this finally? A belated but futile bid for sainthood? You must be kidding? Like Jean says, your head's on a swivel, always has been.

Gus came to a stop, used his free arm to grab me by the shoulder, and turned me around so we were standing face to face. He put down his suitcase and let his arms hang at his sides.

You know, Rob, sometimes you push just a little too hard. He clenched and unclenched his fists. Sometimes you can be a first-class prick, especially with your holier-than-thou routine. I think the best thing for both of us is for you to keep your nose out of my business.

That works both ways, I said, although my heart wasn't in it, not at all. The old gunfight mentality. Gus and I squared off like this. Such moments were void of heroics, I knew this, yet I couldn't help myself.

The four of us stood outside the doors to our rooms. Across the courtyard, I noticed that someone had parted their curtains and was peering out, obviously trying to determine what all the commotion was about. Gus and

I must have looked a sight. Two grown men standing toe to toe, ready to fight over what had been said, over what, between friends, should have been unsayable. Eric moved between us, gazed up and said, What's going on? Dad? I felt awful. Hopeless. You fall into these situations so quickly, with no effort, then you have to claw your way out, without losing face. Or control. Or both. I could tell Eric was not impressed, even if he didn't yet understand what drove men to stage these fiascos.

Dad?

Gus and I stared at each other. We had inadvertently crossed a line that both of us knew should never be crossed, no matter how strong the friendship. But neither of us was prepared to budge. I hadn't meant to be critical, to judge, far from it, but I could see where Gus might take exception to what probably sounded like my taking the moral high ground. On the other hand, I didn't much care for the way he talked in front of Eric, always trying to endear himself with stories and jokes told at someone else's expense. He was right, though, what he did on his own time was his concern. That he caused me to doubt myself and to ponder what increasingly seemed to me to be my limitations was not his problem.

I don't know, son, I said, as far as I can see nothing's going on. Nothing. A misunderstanding. We're all just a bit tired. Not thinking straight about what we're saying. That's all.

I heard the air move overhead and saw bats swoop down into the dim glow cast by the overhead lights.

Then I made an attempt to whistle the theme song from "The Good, The Bad and The Ugly," a film Gus and I had watched together at least three or four times. I put my fist to my mouth to help smother a laugh.

Gus smiled. Do we really look that stupid?

I think so, I said. I think we do.

Jesus!

As quickly as anger had flushed Gus's face, it disappeared. He put one hand on Eric's shoulder and with his other arm pulled Jamie towards him. Your old man's right, Eric, he said. Still, who would have thought? This woman, he said, wouldn't know Claire to speak to her, but through some incredible network they're tapped into, probably through coffee klatches, she knows Claire by name.

There's the rub, Jamie said. Today's secret is tomorrow's gossip. Back home, folks have that down to a science.

Precisely, Gus said and smiled. You may not believe me, but this is the first time since Claire and I were married—that's twenty-seven years ago now—that I've looked at another woman with the thought of having a sexual liaison.

I wasn't prepared to rehash the situation, not yet, so I nodded. What Gus believed about himself and Claire I had no right to challenge.

Really, he said.

I believe you, I said. I was standing in the doorway, holding onto our luggage, when Eric broke free from Gus and came and stood by my side, half helping to grip one of the suitcases, half holding on to my hand.

Then he released his fingers, moved in between me and the suitcase and put his arm around my waist.

You okay? he said.

This was not a question I expected. Fine, I said, just fine.

As I turned to go into the room, I said to Gus, By the way, I doubt it would take a very sophisticated organization to track our movements.

Ain't that the truth! he said and laughed. Then he turned to Jamie and said, Rob's agreed to join us on tonight's tour of duty, so we'll see then who's the old man.

This would be the first night I hadn't stayed behind in the room with Eric, but Gus and Jamie insisted I needed to get out.

Armed with a coke and a bag of potato chips, Eric threw himself across the bed, in front of the TV. I told him to turn out the lights at eleven, that I expected him to obey my instructions, that I'd check back on him before midnight, which I never did. He was probably asleep by then, but I felt at the time, and feel now, guilty for not following up on my word. I think we all have a way of knowing when someone is unreliable. I didn't want Eric to feel that way about me, but as Jean was quick to point out, I was someone always willing to be led astray. You have no will power, she said, no backbone.

Gus, Jamie and I walked across the street to the tavern we'd seen as we drove in to the motel. As soon as we stepped through the doors, Jamie took one look around at the sombreros and framed posters of Mexico

City, Puerto Vallarta, Cancun, Acapulco and Mazatlan hung on the walls and said, Mexico, as I always envisioned it.

They've spared no expense on the decor, Gus said, transports you right out of Rock Springs, that's for sure.

We walked over the planked dance floor that split the room in half to the large horseshoe-shaped bar that extended out from the back wall. The only windows I could see were in the doors through which we'd just entered. Beyond the pool table at the far end of the room was a red exit sign. For some reason, all the lights except those above the bar were orange, perhaps to give the illusion of heat during the winter months.

Guaranteed to drive you to drink, Gus said.

Overhead dark beams crisscrossed the ceiling and a couple of fans stirred the cigarette smoke. Music—mostly western mixed in with a bit of R&B and rock—spilled into the room from speakers.

The *pièce de résistance*, though, I said, are the black-and-white photographs of celebrities partying. Reminds me of family and home.

Before the bartender, a Latino with pitch-black hair, brown eyes and tattoos up both arms, could ask him for ID, Jamie had plunked his passport down on the bar. This had become a running joke on the trip. We would check Jamie into a place for the children's fare, and less than an hour later he'd be in some bar.

Hey, honey!

Gus and I looked up. Opposite us, across the open space of the horseshoe, a large woman, who I was certain was wearing a red wig, waved in our direction.

No, no, not you two retreads, she said, the young one.

Jamie smiled at us and turned to her.

You a virgin? She giggled and then coughed.

Watch out for Mama, said the bartender when he brought us our beers, she'll go after him, and he nodded at Jamie. Like a pit bull, he said, laughing and flashing his teeth. She loves the young ones.

Hey, she said, I asked you if you're a virgin?

Jamie looked at Gus and me. My God, he said, I'm being hustled by the oldest hooker in Wyoming. We've come to a significant moment in our friendship, he said.

Yes, Gus and I said almost in unison.

The woman held her hand to her ear.

He is, Gus shouted, and he's looking for the company of a mature woman.

I understand. She climbed off her stool and made her way around the bar, never taking her eyes from Jamie. I understand. You and me is going to dance up a storm tonight, she said. As she approached, we could see that her eyebrows were two narrow lines, her lips bright red and large, her eyes floating in blue chalk. She grabbed Jamie's hand and pulled him out onto the dance floor. She wasn't quite as old as we thought and moved with a grace—like bourbon over ice, Gus said—that I think surprised even Jamie.

While they danced, an older man wearing a dark brown suit—slightly soiled—dark glasses and a straw hat came and stood between Gus and me. He took a cigarette from his mouth and said, Has Carlos warned you? A puff of smoke accompanied his words.

Gus and I looked at each other because neither of us

was sure we'd heard correctly. To my ear his voice sounded like it had been ground through a pepper mill, his accent thick and southern.

I'm Archie, he said. We shook hands. I said, has Carlos warned you to keep the young 'un away from Mama?

We nodded.

Well, best heed his word, Archie said. She's the devil in drag, as sure as I'm standin' here.

At that moment, after four songs, during which time Mama never let Jamie out of her grip or embrace, Jamie made his escape, but only because Mama couldn't figure out how to dance to the new music. A flamenco piece. She moved, listened, moved again, but her powerful legs fought the rhythm. Jamie slipped away, for the moment, forgotten.

He rushed back and stood next to Archie, who could have passed for Jamie's father. The two, standing side by side, were about the same height, hollow-cheeked and cave-chested. Jamie was white and perspiring. I could have been crushed, you silly buggers, he said. She's bloody mad.

When Archie heard him speak, he said to Jamie, You-all from down my way, I can hear it—I can hear it in the dance of your words.

Just then a different song began to play and Mama came out of her trance, looking for her partner. She came towards us, but Archie stepped in front of Jamie, faced Mama and made a cross with his fingers. Back off, Mama, he said, I'm warning you. I'm taking this one under my wing. At least this was what we thought he said, when we talked the next day about what had happened.

Mama retreated to her stool and said to Gus and me, He's crazy, that old coot, you know that? She paused, smiled, and then laughing, said, Is he a virgin? The young one. Just for my own peace of mind, she said.

We both shrugged.

Meanwhile Jamie and Archie had moved down the bar and appeared engrossed in conversation. I didn't know what to think. Here you had two guys, both half pissed, one with the broadest southern drawl you can imagine, talking to a kid from Lancashire who arguably didn't even speak English, at least not an English any of us understood. I mean, words none of us had ever heard kept popping out of his mouth. And he dropped words from his sentences, as if he were speaking in shorthand. Yet Archie's head nodded, Jamie laughed, and they touched glasses, as if toasting something or other. And while those two talked, the oldest hooker in Wyoming kept trying to get her two bits worth in. Gus said, She's determined to get her man. Got to admire that western spirit.

A while later and with several drinks under his belt, Gus turned to me and said, You know, she's not half bad looking.

I shook my head.

No, seriously. A guy could do worse. And with that he stumbled around the bar, at the same time motioning to Carlos to bring two drinks. Carlos looked at me and said, The light has gone from your partner's eyes. I think he's in danger of losing his way. And we both laughed.

I watched as Gus whispered into Mama's ear. Then

he turned around and navigated his way back, his arms gesturing, waving about his head. You know what that bitch said? She said, You're clearly available, but are you capable?

The next morning, as we drove out of Rock Springs, Gus complained that he felt like his head had been kicked by a mule. He was still sore as hell about Mama's rejection. Jamie praised Gus's spirit and thanked him and Archie for diverting Mama's attention. For the longest time, though, until he got used to Archie's strong accent, he hadn't understood a word the older man had spoken. From the moment the old guy opened his mouth, I could have sworn he was speaking Latin. No doubt, we said and laughed. Puzzled, Jamie looked at us and said, Do him and me even speak the same language? That's what I kept wondering. Bloke were as daft as an old boot, he said. Kept asking me to marry one of his daughters. At least, I think that's what he was proposing. Can't be sure. Wanted me to return to Georgia with him where he claimed to own a small farm. Or bootlegging still. Or both. I figured at best there was only a drop of oil left in his lamp. But all the same, Jamie said, I'm grateful, and gratitude's not to be squandered. Bless you and Archie both, he said to Gus, she was the devil, our Mama. But then you would know better than I, wouldn't you, ol' mate of mine? I'd been saved, he went on, truly saved. A religious experience to be sure, he said.

As I lie here I'm thinking the difference between what passes for spiritual and what defines worldly can be a very fine line. Troy, in Ford's story "Winterkill" asks, "Do you ever just think of just doing a criminal thing sometime?" I think we all give that notion some thought. Sometimes what we do borders on the criminal, without intention. As far as I knew, Jamie and Gus hadn't done anything illegal and I wasn't sure I wanted to do anything illegal. I certainly didn't want Eric to witness anything criminal. Perhaps we'd changed a few lives in Cheyenne and Rock Springs, and provided some harmless entertainment in the process. What I did know was that I wanted out of a rut. I wanted a conversion of sorts. I was certain of that.

On the drive from Boise down to the coast, I was filled with optimism. I felt an exhilaration as we approached the sea. Even the wind surfers on the Columbia stirred my blood; the red, blue, yellow sails skimming across the river; the chop; the toiling green glass cutting and swirling through the gorge. The waters rushing, much as we were, to get elsewhere. Somewhere.

Gus was driving and my body told me it wanted to sleep, but the anticipation of reaching the river delta below, the lushness of forest and bottom country, coupled with memories from the last two nights in bars, kept me awake—much as these recollections do tonight as I lie here in the dark.

I'm a person who likes to live my life largely as it unfolds for me—casting back rarely solves anything and projecting forward is begging disappointment. And generally speaking, in spite of what I'm doing here, I don't like to examine my life too closely. I think I fear

I might think poorly of myself. What I worry about most is that I've missed something, that my life is empty like those huge spaces we passed through. I worry that I'm not paying attention to everything that's going on around me.

To my thinking, this is true for most men. We don't know how to treat women, how to talk to them, how to listen to them. We try. God knows we try, but we always screw up. As we do in most of our relationships. In my case, this is true as much for Eric as it is for Jean. Occasionally I glimpse possibilities. But as careful as we try to be, I'm not sure there are enough words for us to say what we really mean, whether male or female. Father or son.

As we drove out of Portland, Eric said from the back seat, Where's Mum?

Home by now, I said. Probably. Or flying home. She could be on the ferry. Any of those is possible.

Don't you know? he asked.

We were on a bridge, crossing over the Columbia. Gus pointed at a plane that looked like it was coming in for a landing on the river, its landing gear released and the engines already throttling back only a few hundred feet above us.

Not really, I said. Why? You worried?

No, Eric said, just wondering where she's at.

Up ahead two large yellow arrows flashed and guided three lanes of traffic into one. We slowed down, almost coming to a stop. As we inched along, bumper to bumper, I turned to look at him. He stared back at me, a sideways-and-up look, through his eyelashes. You're sure she's headed home, though? he said.

I'm sure, I said. When I felt a tug on the steering wheel, I spun back to see where I was going. For Christ's sake, Gus said, watch the road.

I'd come pretty close to sideswiping the car next to me. A woman driving a small sports car and wearing dark glasses and a golf visor yelled at me and then tapped her temple with her forefinger. I tried smiling and when that didn't work I rolled down the window to say I was sorry, but she seized the opportunity to cut in front of me, clearly anxious to put some distance between herself and the dazed menace beside her.

Eric had always wanted to know things for himself. That was the certainty of it for him. His knowing. And my word was not enough, was not something on which to base his knowledge, at least not yet.

And the motel we'd stayed in last night hadn't helped matters. All through the night I'd heard men and women coming and going. In the morning it was obvious Eric had not got much sleep. At breakfast he put his hand on Gus's arm and said, Was that one of those places you were telling Jamie and me about?

Gus nodded and said, Not quite. Similar. It was noisy, though. That place was jumping most of the night. A lot of the old in out.

I looked at Gus, at the big grin plastered all over his face, and wondered what the hell he'd been telling Eric.

He misses his mum, Gus said, looking at me. You can't blame him for that, especially after spending a couple of weeks with the likes of us. He laughed and gave me thumbs-up.

I wanted to smack him in the mouth. He should have known how important it was for me to gain Eric's trust.

I switch the light back on. Jean moans and rolls over, her black hair trailing across the pillow. Momentarily her eyes blink open, then close. I watch her legs stretch and spread beneath the blankets, watch her arms fall back onto the pillow, as if she is waiting for me. But at that very moment all I want to do is kiss her, nothing more, and tell her how beautiful I think she is, tell her how much I love her, nineteen years down the road; we haven't had that sort of intimacy in some time. In the morning, if she's tired, she'll blame me for her restless night. I pick up Ford's book and flip to the story "Sweethearts." In that story, Bobby says, "I put all my faith in women . . . I see now that was wrong."

If I'd known of this story a few years back, on the trip, I think I might have tried to find a way to say this very same thing to Eric, about most women I'd known. Even about his mother. Not that I wanted to badmouth her, or that she had done anything to deserve such ill will, but I wanted him to believe in me. This seemed to me important then, if our time together was to have any meaning at all. If the talking we'd done was to amount to anything in his life.

I close the book and glance at the cover blurb which says, " . . . *Rock Springs* is the very poetry of realism . . . Ford . . . is a perfect ventriloquist." Perhaps this is true. As I see it, writing is really little more than the recalling of a life—one way of correcting or illuminating the mistakes. A second chance. The way we see ourselves. This doesn't mean you have the right to delete or deny what makes you feel uncomfortable. What you're wrong about. Or revise the image you present to the world. Denial accomplishes nothing. You go with what you think you know. Or don't know, I guess.

These days, when Jean and I are both awake and reading in bed, we seldom say much of anything to each other, but when we do talk we often don't mean what we say. We're testing each other. In my new incarnation, I'm the aggressive one, she's the injured party. Blameless. At least that's the way most of our conversations appear to work themselves out. Privately I tend to think blame should be shared, apportioned fifty-fifty. Each time we negotiate one of these scenes, we each push the other a bit further, to find the breaking point, which, of course, neither of us wants to find. After all, we do love each other. I think. I hesitate only because I'm not sure either of us knows what that word means anymore, although early in our marriage we were both pretty confident we knew exactly what it meant. At risk of stating the obvious, attitudes change—youthful invincibility is replaced by the transparency of middle-aged doubt and pragmatism.

Now, as I think about Ford, I sense he would agree with that, with much of what I've said. Or at least his characters would. I'm not sure what Ford, himself, thinks, as I shouldn't. I suspect his people have as little or as much to do with him as my friends and family have to do with me. We have both had a connection to real estate which of all occupations is commerce built on temporality. And a degree of distrust. The sun always burns a hole into a new day, that's the motto I've come to live by.

I put the book down, get off the bed and turn down the covers. I crawl in where I can feel Jean's warmth wrap around me like a skin, like a body we share—where I can smell her perfume, her sweat—scents that have become familiar and beguiling. I reach back and flick off the light. The point is, you don't know what happens when the lights go out, what the body curled up beside you does in the wee hours of the night, what the person beside you dreams. I'm tempted to add that this is especially true about what men know about women. These days that's a topic pretty much considered off limits, taboo, which to be honest doesn't hold much sway with me. But, if pressed, on the basis of my own experience I would have to say I have no evidence to argue the contrary—we're as blind and pigheaded as ever. Sometimes I think the solution is simple—all we have to do is cause as little inconvenience as possible for each other.

As my eyes adjust to the moonlight filtering through the blinds into the room, I can see where Jean's hips curve and rise beside me. I imagine what it would be like to be pinned under her, to bite the inside of her legs, to run my tongue along her thighs. She would tremble. I imagine my fingers circling her belly, lightly, probing. Embarrassed, I reach over and run the back of my hand down her cheek. I don't want to wake her.

As for Eric, he'll have to work out matters for himself, as much as I'd hoped to help guide him towards self-discovery. There is no way round this, no safety net, no magic. There are no glib answers. There is only our unqualified faith in love and our acceptance of the absolute uniqueness of every person on the planet, regardless of sex. My own failure to live up to this ideal places me solidly within a continuum that's doomed. Perhaps Eric's generation will do better, will be that much the wiser, although I have my doubts. The dinosaur doesn't appear to have taught us much. Rogue meteorites are still on the loose out there in space, waiting for their moment. We carve the same circles out of time. The point is, I don't know why most people, let alone women, do what they do.

This is something I'd like to talk over with Jean, but for now I lie in the dark and try to harmonize my breathing with hers.

Pick Me Up at Four

The interior is another country. Desert and lakes, blue jewels, sapphires perhaps, yes, why not sapphires, reflected in the sky. The earth is a white heat in summer, the sun blazing a trail across burnt bodies.

At dusk, I walk the streets in search of a breeze off the water.

Each night I draw her face, her moods, trace directions I've only dreamt. I imagine how I will fit into her, how she will hold me inside. When I wake she is gone. Visitors, I muse, are supposed to take their leave.

But in the morning, she is there again at the table, unexpected. She walks in and takes a seat opposite me. Her eyes are a clear, pale blue. No one was supposed to join me. I'm a little surprised, but pleased for the company. Her yellow blouse is filled with sunshine.

She looks at me and says, Would you rather I left?

I pour her a cup of tea. No, please, stay, I say. Stay.

Drink your tea and listen to the music, which I want to tell her is no match for the music of her own voice.

What do you want from me? she asks.

I don't want her to know that I haven't the slightest idea what I want from her, but I panic and speak anyway.

For you to be here, I say, that's enough.

If it were possible I would ask you to fetch my black silk dress and stockings and hang them on the line to dry, she says. I love the scent and touch of a fresh breeze, the warmth of the summer sun on my skin.

Her smile—she always smiles—gives me comfort. Her painted toenails excite me. These days I invariably feel awkward around those I don't know well. Her legs are long, scissored at the knee. Quite seductive. Thoughts I am not supposed to have, I have.

Come to me, she says.

I want to go to her, but I feel lethargic, weighted down. I remain seated on the floor, my legs crossed, my chin resting in the palms of my hands. From outside I hear cars and trucks rumble by. The bark of a dog.

I could weep.

The eggshell is an oddly spherical void. Not a planet. Not a skull. Although the absence of something in both disturbs all mothers. Everyone is homeless at such moments, she says, as you have been now for far too long.

When I stand and begin to protest, she pulls me down and holds me in her arms, her hips arching towards me.

It is what I have become used to, I say. Lost for language, for words that used to come to me so easily. For stories I planned to write. I'm clumsy now when I speak, tripping as I do when I walk along a rocky beach. Or climb a mountain trail, high into an alpine meadow. I have become used to the ease of sidewalks.

Give me a name, she says.

Why?

To know me better. For when we meet again.

I hear a melody which is always there. A murmur of voices in the silence. Speaking over hers. Surrounding her. The song of those who know what she is going through. The dead. Who have heard it all before.

Diana, I say. Yes, Diana will do. I watch her eyes to see if I have made a mistake. To see if she is amused or angry. She looks distracted, as if the name suffuses the day with infinite possibilities.

She rises, moves slowly towards the French doors, the glass of each separated pane reflecting back a part of her.

Diana, she says, I like that. She opens one of the doors, turns and says, You have so much to learn, so much to gain.

I walk the streets late into the night, recalling her voice. Her hips. Nothing distracts me. Beautiful young women lean against their will to be here. The sound of a saxophone rises from a cellar. Winds up the stairs. Scales the sky.

Acknowledgements

Some of these stories previously appeared in different form in the following magazines: "The Plimsoll Line" in *The Malahat Review*, Victoria, B.C. and "The Garden" as "Enchantment and Other Demons" in *Meanjin* (Australia). "The Last Time We Talked" appeared in the *Bridport Prize Anthology* (England) and as a chapbook published for the Hawthorne Society by Reference West, Victoria, B.C., and "Shade" in the anthology *Rainshadow: Stories From Vancouver Island*.

For their advice and encouragement during the writing of these stories over the years, I am indebted to several friends: Bob Kroetsch, Cynthia Cecil, Katharina and Jonathan Rout, Joe Rosenblatt, Cassandra Pybus, Gary Geddes, Linda Martin, Keith Harrison and Markus Mueller. In particular, I'm grateful to Ursula Vaira and Carol Windley for their indispensable comments and their unfailing attention to detail. And I owe special thanks to my editor and friend, Jay Connolly (and to Mozer, without whom Jay would not be possible), and to my wife, Pat, for their patience, counsel and inspiration. My children have always tolerated my work habits and tidal moods.

Along the way a few teachers shared with me their love of literature and books, none more so than Professor Philip Pinkus to whom I owe a special debt of gratitude.

Also to David Johnston and Scott Colbourne who saw merit in these stories.

And I thank the Canada Council and the British Columbia Arts Council for their support during the writing of these stories.

Ron Smith was born in Vancouver, BC, in 1943, and attended UBC and the University of Leeds. From 1971 to 1998, he taught English and Creative Writing at Malaspina University-College in Nanaimo, and between 1987 and 1990 was the Fiction Editor for Douglas & McIntyre. His fiction and poetry have been published in magazines in Australia, Canada, England, Italy, Jugoslavia and the States. The author of three books of poetry and a play, he lives with his family in Lantzville on Vancouver Island.